Penguin Books
Penguin Modern Stories 4

D0784771

Penguin
Modern
Stories 4

Edited by Judith Burnley

Penguin Books

Penguin Books Ltd, Harmondsworth,
Middlesex, England
Penguin Books Australia Ltd, Ringwood,
Victoria, Australia

First published in book form in Great Britain
by Penguin Books Ltd 1970

'The Talking Trees' originally appeared in *Playboy Magazine*
copyright © 1968 by H.H. Publishing Co. Inc.;
'A Dead Cert' © Sean O'Faolain, 1969; 'A Satisfactory Settlement'
© Nadine Gordimer, 1970; 'Abroad' © Nadine Gordimer, 1968;
'A Man of Mystery', 'The Political Education of Clarissa
Forbes', 'The Beauty Contest' © Shiva Naipaul, 1970

Made and printed in Great Britain by
C. Nicholls & Company Ltd
Set in Monotype Baskerville

This book is sold subject to the condition that
it shall not, by way of trade or otherwise, be lent,
re-sold, hired out, or otherwise circulated without
the publisher's prior consent in any form of
binding or cover other than that in which it is
published and without a similar condition
including this condition being imposed on the
subsequent purchaser

Contents

Introduction

'After you've written a story, you must never, in a state of wild excitement, read it to someone else; don't rush to break the great news that you've given birth. This is not so easy. It takes a lot of effort to keep from rushing next door and reading it, to let it lie for a while and then take a fresh look at it . . .' Isaac Babel illustrates his own comment on the euphoric behaviour of writers in his story INSPIRA-TION at the end of this collection.

Readers need have no such restraint. Sean O'Faolain, Nadine Gordimer and Shiva Naipaul bring news of three very different worlds which are not only Ireland, Africa and the West Indies, but also the stranger private worlds in each writer's head. All these stories are published here for the first time in this country.

Sean O'Faolain

The Talking Trees

There were four of them in the same class at The Red Abbey, all under fifteen. They met every night in Mrs Coffey's sweetshop at the top of the Victoria Road to play the fruit machine, smoke fags and talk about girls. Not that they really talked about them – they just winked, leered, nudged one another, laughed, grunted and groaned about them, or said things like 'See her legs?' 'Yaroosh!' 'Wham!' 'Ouch!' 'Ooof!' or 'If only, if only!' But if anybody had said, 'Only what?' they would not have known precisely what. They knew nothing precisely about girls, they wanted to know everything precisely about girls, there was nobody to tell them precisely all the things they wanted to know about girls and that they thought they wanted to do with them. Aching and wanting, not knowing, half guessing, they dreamed of clouds upon clouds of fat, pink, soft, ardent girls billowing towards them across the horizon of their future. They might just as well have been dreaming of pink porpoises moaning at their feet for love.

In the sweetshop, the tall glass jars of coloured sweets shone in the bright lights. The one-armed fruit machine went zing. Now and again, girls from Saint Monica's came in to buy sweets, giggle roguishly and overpointedly ignore them. Mrs Coffey was young, buxom, fair-haired, blue-eyed and very good-looking. They admired her so much that one night when Georgie Watchman whispered to them that she had fine bubs, Dick Franks told him curtly not to be so

9

coarse and Jimmy Sullivan said in his most toploftical voice, 'Georgie Watchman, you should be jolly well ashamed of yourself, you are no gentleman,' and Tommy Gong Gong said nothing but nodded his head as insistently as a ventriloquist's dummy.

Tommy's real name was Tommy Flynn, but he was so young that neither he nor they were ever quite sure if he really belonged to the gang at all. To show it, they called him all sorts of nicknames, like Inch because he was so small; Fatty because he was so puppy-fat; Pigeon because he had a chest like a woman; Gong Gong because after long bouts of silence, he had a way of suddenly spraying them with wild bursts of talk like a cross between a fire alarm and a garden sprinkler.

That night, all Georgie Watchman did was to make a rude blubber-lip noise at Dick Franks. But he never again said anything about Mrs Coffey. They looked up to Dick. He was the oldest of them. He had long eyelashes like a girl, perfect manners, the sweetest smile and the softest voice. He had been to two English boarding schools, Ampleforth and Downside, and in Ireland to three, Clongowes, Castleknock and Rockwell, and been expelled from all five of them. After that, his mother had made his father retire from the Indian Civil, come back to the old family house in Cork and, as a last hope, send her darling Dicky to The Red Abbey day school. He smoked a corncob pipe and dressed in droopy plus fours with checkered stockings and red flares, as if he was always just coming from or going to the golf course. He played cricket and tennis, games that no other boy at The Red Abbey could afford to play. They saw him as the typical school captain they read about in English boys' papers like the *Gem* and the *Magnet*, the *Boys' Own Paper*, the *Captain* and *Chums*, which was where they got all those swanky words like Wham, Ouch, Yaroosh, Ooof and Jolly Well. He was their Tom Brown, their Bob Cherry, their Tom Merry, those heroes who were always leading Greyfriars' School or Blackfriars' School to victory on the cricket field amid the cap-tossing huzzas of the juniors and the admiring smiles of visiting parents. It never occurred to them that the *Magnet* or the *Gem* would have seen all four of them as perfect models for some such story as the *Cads of Greyfriars'* or the *Bounders of Blackfriars'*, low types given to secret smoking in the spinneys or drinking in The Dead Woman's Inn. While the rest of the school was practising at the nets, they were cheating at examinations or, worst crime of all, betting on horses with red-faced bookies' touts down from London. They were a quartet of rotters certain to be caned ceremoniously in the last chapter before the entire school and then whistled off at dead of night back to their heartbroken fathers and mothers.

It could not have occurred to them, because these crimes did not exist at The Red Abbey. Smoking? At The Red Abbey, any boy who wanted to was free to smoke himself into a galloping consumption, so long as he did it off the premises, in the jakes or up the chimney. Betting? Brother Julius was always passing fellows sixpence, or even a bob, to put on an uncle's or a cousin's horse at Leopardstown or the Curragh. In the memory of man, no boy at The Red Abbey had ever been caned ceremoniously for anything. Fellows were just leathered all day long for not doing their homework, or playing hooky from school, or giving lip, or fighting in class. And they were leathered hard. Two years ago, Jimmy Sullivan had been given six swingers on each hand with the sharp edge of a meter-long ruler for pouring the contents of an inkwell over Georgie Watchman's head in the middle of a history lesson about the Trojan Wars, in spite of his wailing explanations that he had only done it because he thought Georgie Watchman was a scut and all Trojans were blacks. The only reason they did not drink was that they were too poor. While, as for what the *Magnet* and the *Gem* really meant by 'betting' – which, they dimly understood, was some sort of depravity that no English boy would like to see mentioned in print – hardly a week passed that some brother did not say that a hard problem in algebra, or a leaky pen, or a window that would not open or shut was 'a blooming bugger'.

There was the day when little Brother Angelo gathered half a dozen boys about him at playtime to help him with a crossword puzzle.

'Do any of ye,' he asked, 'know what "notorious conduct" could be in seven letters?'

'Buggery?' Georgie suggested innocently.

'Please be serious!' Angelo said. 'This is about conduct.'

When the solution turned out to be Jezebel, little Angelo threw up his hands, said it must be some queer kind of foreign woman and declared that the whole thing was a bugger. Or there was that other day when old Brother Expeditus started to tell them about the strict lives and simple food of Dominican priests and Trappist monks. When Georgie said, 'No tarts, Brother?' Expeditus had laughed loud and long.

'No, Georgie!' he chuckled. 'No pastries of any kind.'

They might as well have been in school in Arcadia. And every other school about them seemed to be just as hopeless. In fact, they might have gone on dreaming of pink porpoises for years, if it were not for a small thing that Gong Gong told them one October night in the sweetshop. He sprayed them with the news that his sister Jenny had been thrown out of class that morning in Saint Monica's for turning up with a red ribbon in her hair, a mother-of-pearl brooch at her neck and smelling of scent.

'Ould Sister Eustasia,' he fizzled, 'made her go out in the yard and wash herself under the tap; she said they didn't want any girls in their school who had notions.'

The three gazed at one another and began at once to discuss all the possible sexy meanings of notions. Georgie had a pocket dictionary. An ingenious contrivance? An imperfect conception? (*U.S.*) Small wares? Finally, they turned to Mrs Coffey. She laughed, nodded towards two giggling girls in the shop who were eating that gummy kind of block toffee that can gag you for half an hour, and said, 'Why don't you ask *them*?'

Georgie did so, most politely, saying, 'Pardon me, ladies, but do you by any chance happen to have notions?' The two girls stared at each other with cow's eyes, blushed scarlet and fled from the shop, shrieking with laughter. Clearly, a 'notion' was very sexy.

'Georgie!' Dick pleaded. 'You're the only one who knows anything. What in heaven's name is it?'

When Georgie had to confess himself stumped, they knew at last that their situation was desperate.

Up to now, Georgie had always been able to produce some sort of answer, right or wrong, to all their questions. He was the one who, to their disgust, told them what contraception (as he called it) meant. He was the one who had explained to them that all babies are delivered from the navel of the mother. He was the one who had warned them that if a fellow kissed a bad woman, he would get leprosy from head to foot. The son of a head constable, living in the police barracks, he had collected his facts simply by listening as quietly as a mouse to the four other policemen lolling in the dayroom of the barracks with their collars open, reading the sporting pages of the *Freeman's Journal*, slowly creasing their polls, and talking about colts and fillies, cows and calves, bulls and bullocks and 'the mysteerious nachure of all faymale wimmen'. He had gathered a lot of other useful stuff by dutiful attendance since the age of eleven at the meetings and marchings of The Protestant Boys' Brigade, and devoted study of the Bible. And now he was stumped by a nun!

Dick lifted his eyelashes at the three of them, jerked his head and led them out on the pavement.

'I have a plan,' he said quietly. 'I've been thinking of it for some time. Chaps! Why don't we see everything with our own eyes?' And he threw them into excited discussion by mentioning a name. 'Daisy Bolster?'

Always, near every school, there is a Daisy Bolster, whom everybody has heard about and nobody knows. They had all seen her at a distance. Tall, a bit skinny, long legs, dark eyes, lids heavy as the dimmers of a car lamp, prominent white teeth, and her lower lip always looked wet. She could be as old as seventeen. Maybe even eighteen! She wore her hair up. Dick told them that he had met her once at the tennis club with four or five other fellows around her and that she had laughed and winked very boldly all the time. Georgie said that he once heard a fellow in school say she went with boys. Gong Gong bubbled that that was true, because his sister Jenny told him that a girl named Daisy Bolster had been thrown out of school three years ago for talking to a boy outside the convent gate. At this, Georgie flew into a terrible rage.

'You stupid slob!' he roared. 'Don't you know yet that when anybody says a boy and girl are talking to each other, it means they're doing you know what?'

'I don't know you know what,' Gong Gong wailed. 'What what?'

'I heard a fellow say,' Jimmy Sullivan revealed solemnly, 'that she has no father and that her mother is no better than she should be.'

Dick said in disapproving tones that he had once met another fellow who had heard her telling some very daring stories.

'Do you think she would show us for a quid?'

Before they parted on the pavement that night, they were no longer talking about a real girl; for once a girl like that gets her name up, she always ends up as a myth; and for a generation afterwards, maybe more, it is the myth that persists.

'Do you remember,' some old chap will wheeze, 'that girl Daisy Bolster? She used to live up the Mardyke. We used to say she was fast.'

The other old boy will nod knowingly, the two of them will look at each other inquisitively, and neither will admit anything, remembering only the long, dark avenue, dim gas lamps, stars hooked in the trees.

Within a month, Dick had fixed it. Their only trouble after that was to collect the money and to decide whether Gong Gong should be allowed to come with them. Dick fixed that, too, at a final special meeting in the sweetshop.

Taking his pipe from between his lips, he looked speculatively at Gong Gong, who looked up at him with eyes big as plums, trembling between the terror of being told he could come with them and the equal terror of being told that he could not.

'Tell me, Gong Gong,' Dick said politely, 'what, exactly, does your father do?'

'He's a tailor,' Tommy said, blushing a bit at having to confess it, knowing that Jimmy's dad was a bank clerk, that Georgie's was a head constable and that Dick's had been a district commissioner in the Punjab.

'Very fine profession,' Dick said kindly. 'Gentleman's tailor and outfitter. I see. Flynn and Company? Or is it Flynn and Sons? Have I seen his emporium?'

'Ah, no,' Tommy said, by now as red as a radish, 'he's not that sort of a tailor at all, he doesn't build suits, ye know, that's a different trade altogether, he works with me mother at home in Tuckey Street, he lets things in and he lets things out, he's what they call a mender and turner, me brother Turlough had this suit I have on me now before I got it, you can see he's very good at his job, he's a real dab ...'

Dick let him run on, nodding sympathetically – meaning to convey to the others that they really could not expect a fellow to know much about girls if his father spent his life mending and turning old clothes in some side alley called Tuckey Street.

'Do you fully realize, Gong Gong, that we are proposing to behold the ultimate in female beauty?'

'You mean,' Gong Gong whispered, 'she'll only be wearing her nightie?'

Georgie Watchman turned from him in disgust to the fruit machine. Dick smiled on.

'The thought had not occurred to me,' he said. 'I wonder, Gong Gong, where do you get all those absolutely filthy ideas. Do you think, if we three subscribe seventeen and sixpence, that you can contribute half a crown?'

'I could feck it, I suppose.'

Dick raised his eyelashes.

'Feck?'

Gong Gong looked shamefully at the tiles.

'I mean steal,' he confessed.

'Don't they give you any pocket money?'

'They give me three pence a week.'

'Well, we have only a week to go. If you can, what was your word, feck half a crown, you may come.'

The night chosen was a Saturday – her mother always went to town on Saturdays; the time of meeting, five o'clock exactly; the place, the entrance to the Mardyke Walk. On any other occasion, it would have been a gloomy spot for a rendezvous; for this adventure, perfect: a long, tree-lined avenue with a few houses and enclosing walls along one side and, on the other side, the sunken little canal whose deep dyke gave the place its name. Secluded, no traffic allowed inside the gates, complete silence, a place where men came every night to stand with their girls behind the elm trees, kissing and whispering for hours. Dick and Georgie were there on the dot of five. Then Jimmy Sullivan came swiftly loping. From where they stood under a tree just beyond the porter's lodge, shivering with excitement, they could see clearly for only about a hundred yards up the long tunnel of elms lit by the first stars above the boughs, one tawny window streaming across a dark garden and, beyond that, a feeble procession of pendent lamps fading dimly away into the blue November dusk. Within another half hour, the avenue would be pitch black between those meagre pools of light.

Her instructions had been precise. In separate pairs, at

exactly half past five, away up there beyond the last lamp where they would be as invisible as cockroaches, they must gather outside her house.

'You won't be able even to see one another,' she had said gleefully to Dick, who had stared coldly at her, wondering how often had she stood behind a tree with some fellow who would not have been able to see her face.

Every light in the house would be out except for the fanlight over the door.

'Ooh!' she had giggled. 'It will be terribly oohey. You won't hear a sound but the branches squeaking. You must come alone to my door. You must leave the other fellows to watch from behind the trees. You must give two short rings. Once, twice. And then give a long ring and wait.' She had started to whisper the rest, her hands by her sides, clawing her dress in her excitement. 'The fanlight will go out if my mother isn't at home. The door will open slowly. You will step into the dark hall. A hand will take your hand. You won't know whose hand it is. It will be like something out of Sherlock Holmes. You will be simply terrified. You won't know what I'm wearing. For all you'll know, I might be wearing nothing at all!'

He must leave the door ajar. The others must follow him one by one. After that . . .

It was now eleven minutes past five and Gong Gong had not yet come. Already, three women had passed up the Mardyke carrying parcels, hurrying home to their warm fires, forerunners of the home-for-tea crowd. When they had passed out of sight, Georgie growled, 'When that slob comes, I'm going to put my boot up his backside.'

Dick, calmly puffing his corncob, gazing wearily up at the stars, laughed tolerantly and said, 'Now, Georgie, don't be impatient. We shall see all! We shall know all!'

Georgie sighed and decided to be weary, too.

'I hope,' he drawled, 'this poor frail isn't going to let us down!'

For three more minutes, they waited in silence, and then

Jimmy Sullivan let out a cry of relief. There was the small, round figure hastening towards them along the Dyke Parade from one lamp-post to another.

'Puffing and panting as usual, I suppose,' Dick chuckled. 'And exactly fourteen minutes late.'

'I hope to God,' Jimmy said, 'he has that pound note. I don't know in hell why you made that slob our treasurer.'

'Because he is poor,' Dick said quietly. 'We would have spent it.'

He came panting up to them, planted a black violin case against the tree and began rummaging in his pockets for the money.

'I'm supposed to be at a music lesson, that's me alibi, me father always wanted to be a musician but he got married instead, he plays the cello, my brother Turlough plays the clarinet, me sister Jenny plays the viola, we have quartets, I sold a Haydn quartet for one and six, I had to borrow sixpence from Jenny, and I fecked the last sixpence from me mother's purse, that's what kept me so late . . .'

They were not listening, staring into the puckered hand-kerchief he was unravelling to point out one by one a crumpled half-note, two half crowns, two shillings and a sixpenny bit.

'That's all yeers! And here's mine. Six threepenny bits for the quartet. That's one and six. Jenny's five pennies and two ha'pence. That makes two bob. And here's the tanner I just fecked from me mother's purse. That makes my two and sixpence.'

Eagerly, he poured the mess into Dick's hands. At the sight of the jumble, Dick roared at him.

'I told you, you bloody little fool, to bring a pound note!'

'You told me to bring a pound.'

'I said a pound note. I can't give this dog's breakfast to a girl like Daisy Bolster.'

'You said a pound.'

They all began to squabble. Jimmy Sullivan shoved Gong Gong. Georgie punched him. Dick shoved Georgie.

Jimmy defended Georgie with, 'We should never have let that slob come with us.'

Gong Gong shouted, 'Who's a slob?' and swiped at him.

Jimmy shoved him again, so that he fell over his violin case, and a man passing home to his tea shouted at them, 'Stop beating that little boy at once!'

Tactfully, they cowered. Dick helped Gong Gong to his feet. Georgie dusted him lovingly. Jimmy retrieved his cap, put it back crookedly on his head and patted him kindly. Dick explained in his best Ampleforth accent that they had merely been having a trifling discussion and 'our young friend here tripped over his suitcase'. The man surveyed them dubiously, growled something and went on his way. When he was gone, Georgie pulled out his pocketbook, handed a brand-new pound note to Dick and grabbed the dirty jumble of cash.

Dick at once said, 'Quick, march! Two by two!' and strode off ahead of the others, side by side with Tommy and his crooked cap and his dusty violin case, into the deepening dusk.

They passed nobody. They heard nothing. They saw only the few lights in the sparse houses along the left of the Mardyke. On the other side was the railed-in dike stream, but that made no more noise than a canal. When they came in silence to the sudden, wide expanse of the cricket field, the sky dropped a blazing veil of stars behind the outfield nets. When they passed the gates of the railed-in public park, locked for the night, utter darkness returned between old high walls to their left and overgrown laurels glistening behind the tall railings on their right. Here Tommy stopped dead, looked fearfully towards the laurels.

'What's up with you?' Dick snapped at him.

'I hear a noise, my father told me once how a man murdered a woman in there for her gold watch, he said men do terrible things like that because of bad women, he said that that man was hanged by the neck in Cork

Jail, he said that was the last time the black flag flew on top of the jail, I don't want to go on!'

Dick peered at the phosphorescent dial of his watch and strode ahead, staring at the next feeble lamp hanging from its black iron arch. Tommy had to trot to catch up with him.

'We know,' Dick said, 'that she has long legs. Her breasts will be white and small.'

'I won't look!' Tommy moaned.

'Then don't look!'

Panting, they hurried on past the corrugated iron building that had once been a roller-skating rink and was now empty and abandoned. After the last lamp, the night was impenetrable, but presently a house rose slowly to their left against the starlight. It was square, tall, solid, brick-fronted, three-storeyed and jet-black against the stars, except for its half-moon fanlight. They walked a few yards past it and halted, panting, behind a tree. The only sound was the squeaking of a branch over their heads. Looking backward, they saw Georgie and Jimmy approaching under the last lamp. Looking forward, they saw a brightly lit tram, on its way outward from the city, pass the far end of the tunnel, briefly light its maw and black it out again. Beyond that lay wide country fields and the silent river. Dick said, 'Tell them to follow me if the fanlight goes out,' and disappeared.

Alone under the tree, backed by the park, Tommy looked across to where the far heights of Sunday's Well gleamed with the eyes of a thousand suburban houses. He clasped his fiddle case before him like a shield. He had to force himself not to run away towards where another bright tram would rattle him back to the city. Suddenly, he saw the fanlight go out. Strings in the air throbbed and faded. Was somebody playing a cello? His father bowed over his cello, jacket off, shirt sleeves rolled up, entered the Haydn; beside him, Jenny waited, chin sideward over her viola, bosom lifted, bow poised, the tendons of her frail wrist hollowed by the lamplight; Turlough, facing them, lipped a thinner reed; his mother sat shawled by the fire, tapping the beat with her toe.

Georgie and Jimmy joined him.

'Where's Dick?' Georgie whispered urgently.

'Did I hear music?' he gasped.

Georgie vanished, and again the strings came and faded. Jimmy whispered, 'Has she a gramophone?' Then they could hear nothing but the faint rattle of the vanished tram. When Jimmy slid away from him, he began to race madly up into the darkness, and then stopped dead halfway to the tunnel's end. He did not have the penny to pay for the tram. He turned and raced as madly back the way he had come, down past her house, down to where the gleam of the laurels hid the murdered woman, and stopped again. He heard a rustling noise. He looked back, thought of her long legs and her small white breasts and found himself walking heavily back to her garden gate. He entered the path, fumbled for the dark door, pressed against it, felt it slue open under his hand, stepped cautiously into the dark hallway, closed the door, saw nothing, heard nothing, stepped onward and fell clattering on the tiles over his violin case.

A door opened. He saw firelight flicker on shining shinbones and bare knees. Fearfully, his eyes moved upward. She was wearing gym knickers. Then he saw only – two small birds, white, beaked, soft, rosy-tipped. Transfixed by joy, he stared and stared at them. Her black hair hung over her narrow shoulders. She laughed down at him with white teeth and wordlessly gestured him to get up and come in. He faltered after her white back and stood inside the door. The only light was from the fire.

Nobody heeded him. Dick stood by the corner of the mantelpiece, one palm flat on it, his other hand holding his trembling corncob. He was peering coldly at her. His eyelashes almost met. Georgie lay sprawled in a chintzy armchair on the other side of the fire, wearily flicking the ash from a black cigarette into the fender. Opposite him, Jimmy Sullivan sat on the edge of a chair, his elbows on his knees, his eyeballs sticking out as if he had just swallowed something hard and raw. Nobody said a word. She stood in the centre of the carpet, looking guardedly from one to the other of them out of her hooded eyes, her thumbs inside the elastic of her gym knickers, ready to press them down over her hips. When Georgie suddenly whispered, 'The seventh veil!' he at once wanted to batter them all over their heads with his fiddle case, to shout at her to stop, to shout at them that they had seen everything, to shout that they must look no more. Instead, he lowered his head so that he saw nothing but her bare feet. Her last ugly garment slid to the carpet. He heard three long gasps, became aware that Dick's pipe had fallen to the floor, that Georgie had started straight up, one fist lifted as if he was going to strike her. Jimmy had covered his face with his hands.

A coal tinkled from the fire to the fender. With averted eyes, he went to it, knelt before it, wet his fingers with his spittle, as he had often seen his mother do, deftly dropped the coal back on the fire and remained so for a moment, watching it light again. Then he sidled back to his violin case, walked out into the hall, flung open the door on a sky of stars and straightway started to race the whole length of the Mardyke, from pool to pool of light, in three gasping spurts.

After the first spurt, he stood panting until his heart stopped hammering. He heard a girl laughing softly behind a tree. Just before his second halt, he saw ahead of him a man and a woman approaching him arm in arm; but when he came up to where they should have been, they, too, had become invisible. Halted, breathing, listening, he heard them murmuring somewhere in the dark. At his third, panting rest, he heard an invisible girl say, 'Oh no, oh no!' and a man's urgent voice say, 'But yes, but yes!' He felt that behind every tree there were kissing lovers, and ran without stopping until he had emerged from the

Mardyke among the bright lights of the city. Then, he was in his own street, the sweat cooling on his forehead, standing outside the shuttered plumber's shop above which they lived. Slowly he climbed the bare stairs to their floor and their door. He paused for a moment to look up through the bare window at the stars, opened the door and went in.

Four heads around the supper table turned to look inquiringly at him. At one end of the table, his mother sat wearing her blue apron. At the other end, his father sat in his rolled-up shirt sleeves, as if he had only just laid down the pressing iron. Turlough gulped his food. Jenny was smiling mockingly at him. She had the red ribbon in her hair and the mother-of-pearl brooch at her neck.

'You're bloody late!' his father said crossly. 'What the hell kept you? I hope you came straight home from your lesson. What way did you come? Did you meet anybody or talk to anybody? You know I don't want any loitering at night. I hope you weren't cadeying with any blackguards? Sit down, sir, and eat your supper. Or did your lordship expect us to wait for you? What did you play tonight? What did Professor Hartmann give you to practise for your next lesson?'

He sat in his place. His mother filled his plate and they all ate in silence.

Always the questions! Always talking and talking at him! They never let him alone for a minute. His hands sank. He stared at his greasy plate. She was so lovely. So white. So lovely. His mother said gently, 'You're not eating, Tommy. Are you all right?'

He said, 'Yes, yes, I'm fine, Mother.'

Like birds. Like stars. Like music.

His mother said, 'You are very silent tonight, Tommy. You usually have a lot of talk after you've been to Professor Hartmann. What are you thinking of?'

'They were so beautiful!' he blurted.

'What was so bloody beautiful?' his father rasped. 'What are you blathering about?'

'The stars,' he said hastily.

Jenny laughed. His father frowned. Silence returned.

He knew that he would never again go back to the sweetshop. They would only want to talk and talk about her. They would want to bring everything out into the light, boasting and smirking about her, taunting him for having run away. He would be happy forever if only he could walk every night of his life up the dark Mardyke, hearing nothing but a girl's laugh from behind a tree, a branch squeaking and the far-off rattle of a lost tram; walk on and on, deeper into the darkness, until he could see nothing but one tall house whose fanlight she would never put out again. The doorbell might ring, but she would not hear it. It might be answered, but not by her. She would be gone. He had known that ever since he heard her laughing softly by his side as he ran away with her forever between those talking trees.

Sean O'Faolain

A Dead Cert

Whenever Jenny Rosse came up to Dublin, for a shopping spree, or a couple of days with the Ward Union Hunt, or to go to the Opera, or to visit some of her widespread brood of relations in or around the city, or to do anything at all just to break the monotony of what she would then mockingly call 'my life in the provinces', the one person she never failed to ring was Oweny Flynn; and no matter how busy Oweny was in the courts or in his law chambers he would drop everything to have a lunch or a dinner with her. They had been close friends ever since he and Billy Rosse – both of them then at The King's Inn – had met her together twelve or thirteen years ago after a yacht race at The Royal Saint George. Indeed they used to be such a close trio that, before she finally married Billy and buried herself in Cork, their friends were always laying bets on which of the two she would choose, and the most popular version of what happened in the end was that she let them draw cards for her. 'The first man,' she had cried gaily, 'to draw the ace of hearts!' According to this account the last card in the pack was Billy's, and before he turned it she fainted. As she was far from being a fainter this caused a great deal of wicked speculation about which man she had always realized she wanted. On the other hand one of her rivals said that she had faked the whole thing to get him.

This Saturday afternoon in October she and Oweny had

25

finished a long, gossipy lunch at the Shelbourne, where she always stayed whenever she came up to Dublin. ('I hate to be tied to my blooming relatives!') They were sipping their coffee and brandy in two deep, saddleback armchairs, the old flowery chintzy kind that the Shelbourne always provided. The lounge was empty and, as always after wine, Oweny had begun to flirt mildly with her, going back over the old days, telling her, to her evident satisfaction, how lonely it is to be a bachelor of thirty-seven ('My life trickling away into the shadows of memory!'), and what a fool he had been to let such a marvellous lump of a girl slip through his fingers, when, all of a sudden, she leaned forward, and tapped the back of his hand like a dog pawing for still more attention.

'Oweny!' she said. 'I sometimes wish my husband would die for a week.'

For a second he stared at her in astonishment. Then, in a brotherly kind of voice, he said, 'Jenny! I hope there's nothing wrong between you and Billy?'

She tossed her red head at the very idea.

'I'm as much in love with Billy as ever I was! Billy is the perfect husband. I wouldn't change him for worlds.'

'So I should have hoped,' Oweny said, dutifully, if a bit stuffily. 'I mean, of all the women in the world you must be one of the luckiest and happiest that ever lived. Married to a successful barrister. Two splendid children. How old is Peter now? Eight? And Anna must be ten. There's a girl who is going to be a breaker of men's hearts and an engine of delight. Like,' he added, remembering his role, 'her beautiful mother. And you have that lovely house at Silverspring. With that marvellous view down the Lee ...'

'You can't live on scenery!' she interposed tartly. 'And there's a wind on that river that'd cool a tomcat!'

'A car of your own. A nanny for the kids. Holidays abroad every year. No troubles or trials that I ever heard of. And,' again remembering his duty, 'if I may say so, every time we meet, you look younger, and,' he plunged daringly, 'more desirable than ever. So, for God's sake, Jenny Rosse, what the hell on earth are you talking about?'

She turned her head to look out pensively at the yellowing sun glittering above the last, trembling, fretted leaves of the trees in the Green, while he gravely watched her, admiring the way its light brought out the copper gold of her hair, licked the flat tip of her cocked nose and shone on her freckled cheek that had always reminded him of peaches and cream, and 'No,' he thought, 'not a pretty woman, not pretty-pretty, anyway I never did care for that kind of prettiness, she is too strong for that, too much vigour. I'm sure she has poor old Billy bossed out of his life!' And he remembered how she used to sail her waterwag closer to the wind than any fellow in the yacht club, and how she used to curse like a trooper if she slammed one into the net, always hating to lose a game, especially to any man, until it might have been only last night that he had felt that aching hole in his belly when he knew that he had lost her for ever. She turned her head to him and smiled wickedly.

'Yes,' she half agreed. 'Everything you say is true but ...'

'But what?' he asked curiously, and sank back into the trough of his armchair to receive her reply.

Her smile vanished.

'Oweny! You know exactly how old I am. I had my thirty-fourth birthday party last week. By the way, I was very cross with you that you didn't come down for it. It was a marvellous party. All Cork was at it. I felt like the Queen of Sheba. It went on until about three in the morning. I enjoyed every single minute of it. But, the next day, I got the shock of my life! I was sitting at my dressing-table brushing my hair.' She stopped dramatically, and pointed her finger tragically at him as if his face were her mirror. 'When I looked out the window at a big, red, grain boat steaming slowly down the river, out to sea,

I stopped brushing, I looked at myself, there and then I said, "Jenny Rosse! You are in your thirty-fifth year. And you've never had a lover!" And I realized that I never could have a lover, not without hurting Billy, unless he obliged me by dying for a week.'

For fully five seconds Oweny laughed and laughed.

'Wait,' he choked, 'until the lads at the club hear this one!'

The next second he was sitting straight up in his arm-chair.

'Jenny,' he said stiffly, 'would you mind telling me why exactly you chose to tell this to me?'

'Aren't you interested?' she asked innocently.

'Isn't it just a tiny little bit unfair?'

'But Billy would never know he'd been dead for a week. At most he'd just think he'd lost his memory or something. Don't you suppose that's what Lazarus thought? Oh! I see what you mean. Well, I suppose yes, I'd have betrayed Billy. That's true enough, isn't it?'

'I am not thinking of your good husband. I am thinking of the other unfortunate fellow when his week would be out!'

'What other fellow? Are you trying to suggest that I've been up to something underhand?'

'I mean,' he pressed on, quite angry now, 'that I refuse to believe that you are mentally incapable of realizing that if you ever did let any other man fall in love with you for even five minutes, not to speak of a whole week, you would be sentencing him to utter misery for the rest of his life.'

'Oh, come off it!' she huffed. 'You always did take things in High C. Why are you so bloody romantic? It was just an idea. I expect lots of women have it only they don't admit it. One little, measly wild oat? It's probably something I should have done before I got married, but,' she grinned happily, 'I was too busy then having a good time. "In the morning sow thy seed and in the evening

withhold not thine hand.'' Ecclesiastes. I learned that at
Alexandra College. Shows you how innocent I was – I
never knew what it really meant until I got married. Of
course, you men are different. You think of nothing
else.'

He winced.

'If you mean me,' he said sourly, 'you know damned
well that I never wanted any woman but you.'

When she laid her hand on his he knew that they both
understood why she had said that about Billy dying for a
week. When he snatched his hand away and she gathered
up her gloves with all the airs of a woman at the end of her
patience with a muff, and strode ahead of him to glare at
the levelling sun outside the hotel, he began to wonder if
he really had understood, and he began to wonder if he
had upset her with all that silly talk about old times. But
a side-glance caught a look in her eyes that was much more
mocking than hurt and at once his anger returned. She had
been doing much more than flirting. Had she just wanted
to challenge him? Close-hauling? Whatever she was
doing she had manoeuvred him into a ridiculous position.
Then he thought, 'Now, she will drive to Cork tonight
and I will never be certain what she really meant.' While
he boggled she started talking brightly about her holiday
plans for the winter. A cover-up? She said she was going
to Gstaad for the skiing next month with a couple of
Cork friends.

'Billy doesn't ski, so he won't come. We need another
man. Would you like to join us? They are nice people. Jim
Chandler and his wife. About our age. You'd enjoy them.'

He said huffily that he was too damned busy; and she
might not know it but some people in the world have to
earn their living; anyway, he was saving up for two weeks'
sailing in the North Sea in June; at which he saw that he
had now genuinely hurt her. ('Dammit, if we really were
lovers this would be our first quarrel!') He forced a
smile.

'Is this good-bye, Jenny? You did say at lunch that you were going to drive home this evening? Shan't I see you again?'

She looked calculatingly at the sun now shivering coldly behind the far leaves.

'I hate going home. I mean so soon. I hate driving alone in the dark. I think I'll just go to bed after dinner and get up bright and early on Sunday morning before the traffic. I'll be back at Silverspring in time for lunch.'

'If you are doing nothing tonight why don't you let me take you to dinner at the Yacht Club?'

She hesitated. Cogitating the long road home?

'Do come, Jenny! They'd all love to see you. It will be like old times. You remember the Saturday night crowds?'

She spoke without enthusiasm.

'So be it. Let's do that.'

She presented her freckled cheek for his parting kiss. In frank admiration he watched her buttocks swaying provocatively around the corner of Kildare Street.

Several times during the afternoon, back in his office, he found himself straying from his work to her equivocal words. Could there, after all, be something wrong between herself and Billy? Could she be growing tired of him? It could happen, and easily: a decent chap, fair enough company, silent, a bit slow, not brilliant even at his own job, successful only because of his father's name and connexions, never any good at all at sport. He could easily see her flying down the Eggli at half a mile a minute, the snow powder leaping from her skis when she would be doing a Christy. But not Billy: he would be down by the railway station paddling around like a duck among the beginners – and he remembered what a hopeless sheep he had always been with the girls, who nevertheless seemed to flock around him all the time, perhaps (it was the only explanation he ever found for it) because he was the sort of shy, fumbling kind of fellow that awakens the maternal instinct in girls. At which he saw her, not as a girl in white shorts dashing on the tennis courts, but as the splendidly mature woman who had turned his face into her mirror by crying along her pointing finger, 'You are in your thirty-fifth year!'

How agile, he wondered, would she now be on the ski-slopes? He rose and stood for a long time by his window, glaring down at the Saturday evening blankness of Nassau Street, and the deserted playing fields of Trinity College, and the small lights of the buses moving through the blueing dusk, until he shivered at the cold creeping through the pane, and felt the tilt of time and the failing year, and in excitement understood her sudden lust.

As always on Saturday nights, once the autumn came and the sailing finished, the lounge and the bar of the club were a cascade of noise and, if he had been alone, he would at once have added his bubble of chatter to it. He stood proudly beside the finest woman in the crowd, covertly watching her smiling around her, awaiting attention from her rout, (What was that great line? *Diana's foresters, gentlemen of the shades, minions of the moon?*) until, suddenly, alerted and disturbed, he found her eyes turning from the inattentive mob to look out unsmilingly to where the lighthouse on the pier's end was writing slow circles on the dusty water of the harbour. He said, 'Jenny, you are not listening to me?' and was bewildered when she whispered, 'But I don't know a single one of these young people!' He pointed out the commodore, whom she should have remembered from the old days. She peered and said, 'Not *that* old man?' He said, 'How could you have forgotten?' The 'old man' had not forgotten as he found when he went to the bar to refresh their drinks.

'Isn't that Jenny Rosse you have there?' he asked Oweny. 'She's putting on weight, bedad! Ah, she did well for herself.'

'How do you mean?' Oweny asked, a bit shortly.

'Come off it. Didn't she marry one of the finest practices in Cork! Handsome is as handsome does, my boy! She backed a dead cert.'

It washed off his back. Jealous old bastard! As he handed her the glass she asked idly, 'Who is that strong looking girl in blue, she is as brown as if she has been sailing all summer?' He looked.

'One of the young set. I think she's George Whitaker's daughter.'

'That nice looking chap in the black tie? He looks the way Billy used to look. Who is he?'

'Saturday nights!' he said impatiently. 'You know the way they bring the whole family, it gives their wives a rest from the cooking.'

It was a relief to lead her into the dining room and to find her mood suddenly change to complete happiness.

'So this,' she laughed, 'is where it all began. And look! The same old paintings. They haven't changed a thing.'

The wine helped, and now safely islanded in their corner, even the families baying cheerfully at one another from table to table, though she got on his nerves by dawdling so long over the coffee, even asking for a second pot, that the maids had cleared every table but theirs, before she revealed her mood by saying:– 'Oweny! Please let's go somewhere else for our nightcap.'

'But where?' he said irritably. 'Some scruffy pub?'

'Or your flat?' she suggested, and his hopes beamed like a water lily. They shrivelled when she stepped out ahead of him into the cold night air, looked up at the three-quarter moon, and then at the Town Hall clock, and said, 'What a stunning night! Oweny, I've changed my mind. Just give me a good strong coffee and I'll drive home right away.'

'So,' he said miserably, 'we squabbled at lunch, and our dinner was a flop.'

She protested that it had been a marvellous dinner;

and wasn't it grand the way nothing had been changed, 'They even still have that old picture of the Duke of Windsor when he was a boy in the navy.' He gave up. He had lost the set. All the way into town she only spoke once.

'We had good times,' she said. 'I could do it all over again.'

'And I suppose change nothing?' he growled.

Her answer was pleasing, but inconclusive – 'Who knows?'

If only he could have her in the witness box, under oath, for fifteen minutes!

In his kitchenette, helping him to make the coffee, she became so full of good spirits (because, he understood dourly, she was about to take off for home) that he thrust an arm about her waist, assaulted her cheek with a kiss as loud as a champagne cork, and said fervently (he had nothing to lose now), 'And I thinking how marvellous it would be if we could be in bed together all night!' She laughed mockingly, handed him the coffee pot, a woman long accustomed to the grappling hook, and led the way with the cups back into his living room. They sat on the small sofa before his coffee table.

'And I'll tell you another thing, Jenny!' he said, 'If I had this flat twelve years ago it might very easily have happened that you would have become my one true love! You would have changed and crowned my whole life.'

Had she heard him? She had let her head roll back on the carved moulding of the sofa and was looking out past him at the moon. Quickly he kissed her mouth. Unstirring she looked back into his eyes, whispered, 'I should not have let you do that,' returned her eyes to the moon, and whispered, 'Or should I?'

'Jenny!' he coaxed. 'Close your eyes, and let's pretend we really are back twelve years ago.'

Her eyelids sank. He kissed her again, very softly, felt her hand creep to his shoulder and impress his kiss, felt her lips fall apart, her hand fall weakly away, desire climb into his throat, and then, he heard her softly moan the disenchanting name. He drew back, rose, and looked helplessly down at her until she opened her eyes, stared uncomprehendingly around her, and looked up at him in startled recognition.

'So,' he said bitterly, 'he did not die even for one minute.'

She laughed wryly, and lightly, and stoically, a woman who would never take anything in a high key, except a five-barred gate or a double-ditch.

'Whenever I dream of having a lover I always find myself at the last moment in my husband's arms.'

She jumped up, snatched her coat and turned furiously on him.

'Why the hell, for God's sake, don't you go away and get married?'

'To have me dreaming about you? Is that what you really want?'

'To put us both out of pain!'

They glared hatefully at one another.

'Please drive me to the Shelbourne. I want to get on the road right away.'

They drove to the Green without a word, she got out, slammed the car door behind her and raced into the hotel. He whirled, drove hell for leather back to the club, killed the end of the night with the last few gossipers, drank far too much and lay awake for hours staring sideways from his pillow over the grey, frosting roofs and countless yellow chimney pots of Dublin.

Past twelve. In her yellow sports Triumph she would tear across the Curragh at seventy and along the two straight stretches before and after Monasterevan. By now she has long since passed through Port Laoise and Abbeyleix where only a few lighted upper storey windows still resisted sleep. From that, for hour after hour, south and south, every village street and small town she passes will be fast asleep, every roadside cottage, every hedge, field and tree, and the whole, widespread moonblanched country pouring past her headlights until she herself gradually becomes hedge, tree, field, greenness and fleeting moon. Hedges, arched branches underlit by her headlights, old demesne walls, a closed garage, a grey church, a lifeless gate-lodge, all motionless until the black rock and ruin of Cashel comes slowly wheeling about the moon. A street lamp falling on a black window makes it still more black. Cars parked beside a kerb huddle from the cold. In Cahir the boarded windows of the old granaries are blind with age, its dull square empty. Her wheeling lights flash the vacant eyes of the hotel, leap the humpbacked bridge, fleck the side of the Norman castle. She is dong seventy again on the level, windy uplands of the Galtee mountains, heedless of the sleep-wrapt plain that slopes for miles and miles away to her left.

Why is she stopping? To rest, to look, to listen? He can see nothing for her to see but a scatter of mushroom farmhouses on the plain, hear nothing but one sleepless dog as far away as the lofty moon. He lights his bedside lamp. Turned half past two. He puts out his light and there are her kangaroo lights, leaping, climbing, dropping, winding, slowing now because of the twisting strain on her arms. She does not see the sleeping streets of Fermoy; only the white signpost marking the remaining miles to Cork. Her red tail-lights disappear and reappear before him every time she winds and unwinds, down to the sleeping estuary of the low-tide Lee, not so much a river as a lough, cold, grey, turbulent and empty. He tears after her as she rolls smoothly westward beside its shining slobland. Before them low, bruised clouds hung over her lighted city, silently awaiting the silent morning.

She brakes to turn in between her white gates, her wheels spit back the gravel, she zooms upward to her house and halts under its staring windows. She switches off the engine, struggles out, stretches her arms high above her head with a long, shivering, happy, outpouring groan, and then, breathing back a long breath, she holds her breasts up to her windows. There is not a sound but the metal of her engine creaking as it cools, and a cold, small wind whispering up from the river. She laughs to see their cat flow like black water around the corner of the house. She leans into the car, blows three long, triumphant horn blasts, and before two windows can light up over her head she has disappeared indoors as smoothly as her cat. And that, at last, it is the end of sleep, where, behind windows gone dark again, she spreads herself for love.

From the Liffey or the Lee neither of them hears the morning seagulls. He wakes unrefreshed to the sounds of late church bells. She half opens her eyes to the flickering light of the river on her ceiling, rolls over on her belly, and stretching out her legs behind her like a satisfied cat dozes off again. He stares for a long time at his ceiling hardly hearing the noise of the buses going by. It is cold. His mind is clear and cold. I know now what she wants. But does she ? Let her lie. For a while longer.

She called me a romantic and she has her own fantasy. She has what she wanted, wants what she cannot have, is not satisfied with what she has got. I have known her for over twelve years and never known her at all. The most adorable woman I ever met. And a slut. If she had married me would she be dreaming now of him? Who was it said faithful women are always pondering on their fidelity, never on their husbands' ? Die for a week ? He chuckled at her joke. Joke ? Or gamble ? Or a dead cert ? If I could make him die for a week it might be a hell of a long week for her. Should I write to her ? I could telephone.

Hello, Jenny! It's me. I just wanted to be sure you got back safely the other night. Why wouldn't I worry ? About anyone as precious as you ? Those frosty roads. Of course it was, darling, a lovely meeting, and we must do it again. No, nothing changes. That's a dead cert. Oh, and Jenny! I nearly forgot. About that skiing bit next month in

Gstaad. Can I change my mind? I'd love to join you. May I? Splendid! Oh, no! Not for that long. Say.... Just for a week?

He could see her hanging up the receiver very slowly.

Nadine Gordimer

A Satisfactory
Settlement

A sagging hulk of an American car, its bodywork like coloured tinfoil that has been screwed into a ball and smoothed out, was beached on the axle of a missing wheel in a gutter of the neighbourhood. Overnight, empty beer cartons appeared against well-oiled wooden gates; out-of-works loped the streets and held converse on corners with nannies in their pink uniforms and houseboys in aprons. In dilapidated outbuildings dating from the time when they housed horses and traps, servants kept all sorts of hangers-on. The estate agent had pointed out that it was one of the quiet old suburbs of Johannesburg where civil servants and university lecturers were the sort of neighbours one had – but of course no one said anything about the natives.

The child was allowed to ride his bicycle on the pavement and he liked to go and look at the car. He and his mother knew none of their neighbours yet, and in the street he simply thought aloud; he said to a barefoot old man in an army greatcoat, 'There's a dead rat by the tree at the corner. I found it yesterday.' And the old man clapped his hands slowly, with the gum-grin of ancients and infants: '*S'bona,* my *baasie* may the Lord bless you, you are big man.' Under one of the silky oaks of the pavement the child said to a man who had been lying all morning in the shade with a straw hat with a paisley band over his eyes,

and a brand-new transistor-radio playing beside his head,
'Did you steal it?'

The man said without moving, 'My friend, I got it in
town.' The furze of beard and moustache were drawn
back suddenly in a lazy yawn that closed with a snap.

'I saw a dead rat there by the corner.'

'The crock's been pushed to Tanner Road.'

'There's a native boy's got a ten transistor.'

His mother was not interested in any of this intelligence.
Her face was fixed in vague politeness, she heard without
listening to what was said, just as he did when she talked
on the telephone: '... no question of signing *anything* whatever until provision's made ... my dear Marguerite, I've
been fooled long enough, you can put your mind at rest ...
only in the presence of the lawyers ... the door in his face,
that's ... cut out the parties he takes to the races every
Saturday, and the flush dinners, then, if he can't afford
to make proper provision ... *and*, I said, I want a special
clause in the maintenance agreement ... medical expenses
up till the age of twenty-one ...'

When his mother was not talking to Marguerite on the
telephone it was very quiet in the new house. It was as if she
were still talking to Marguerite in her mind. She had taken
the white bedside radio from her room in the old house –
daddy's house – to a swop shop and she had brought home a
grey portable typewriter. It stood on the dining table and she
slowly picked out letters with her eyes on the typing manual
beside her. The tapping became his mother's voice, stopping
and starting, hesitantly and dryly, out of her silence. She
was going to get a job and work in an office; he was going
to a new school. Later on when everything was settled, she
said, he would sometimes spend a week-end with daddy.
In the meantime it was the summer holidays and he could
do what he liked.

He did not think about the friends he had played with
in the old house. The move was only across the town, but
for the boy seas and continents might have been between

and the suburb a new country from where Rolf and Sheila were a flash of sun on bicycles on a receding horizon. He could not miss them as he had done when they had been in the house next door and prevented, by some punishment or other, from coming over to play. He wandered in the street; the rat was taken away, but the old man came back again – he was packing and unpacking his paper carrier on the pavement: knotted rags, half-loaf of brown bread, snuff, a pair of boots whose soles grinned away from the uppers, and a metal funnel. The boy suddenly wanted the funnel, and paid the old man fifteen cents for it. Then he hid it in the weeds in the garden so that his mother wouldn't ask where he'd got it.

The man with the radio sometimes called out, 'My friend, where you going?' 'My friend, watch out for the police!'

The boy lingered a few feet off while the man went on talking and laughing, in their own language, with the group that collected outside the house with the white Alsatian.

'Why d'you say that about the policeman?'

The man noticed him again, and laughed. 'My friend, my friend!'

Perhaps the old man had told about the funnel; a funnel like that might cost fifty cents. In a shop. The boy didn't really believe about the policeman; but when the man laughed, he felt he wanted to run away, and laugh back, at the same time. He was drawn to the house with the white Alsatian and would have liked to ride past without hands on the handlebars if only he hadn't been afraid of the Alsatian rushing out to bite the tyres. The Alsatian sat head-on-paws on the pavement among the night watch-man and his friends, but when it was alone behind the low garden wall of the house it screamed, snarled and leapt at the women who went by in slippers and cotton uniforms gaping between the buttons, and yelled '*Voetsak!*' and '*Suka!*' at it. There were also two women who dressed as if they were white, in tight trousers, and had straightened hair and lipstick. One afternoon they had a fight, tearing at each other, sobbing, and swearing in English. The Alsatian went hysterical but the night watchman had him by the collar.

The old car actually got going – even when the wheel was on, there was still the flat battery, and he put down his bike and helped push. He was offered a ride but stood shaking his head, his chest heaving. A young man in a spotless white golf-cap and a torn and filthy sweater wanted to buy his watch. They had been pushing side by side and they sat in the gutter, smiling like panting dogs. 'I pay you five pounds!' The slim, sticky black hand fingered his wrist, on which the big watch sat a bit off-centre.

'But where have you got five pounds?'

'How I can say I buy from you if I can't have five pounds? I will pay five pounds!'

The impossible size of the sum, quoted in old currency, as one might talk wildly of ducats or doubloons, hung in credible bluff between them. He said of his watch: 'I got it for Christmas.' But what was Christmas to the other?

'Five pounds!'

A nanny pushing a white child in a cart called out something in their language. The hand dropped the skinny wrist and a derisive tongue-click made the boy feel himself dismissed as a baby.

He did not play in the garden. His toys all had been brought along but there was no place for them yet; they stood about in his room with the furniture that had been set here or there by the movers. His mother dragged his bed under the window and asked, 'Is that where you want it?' And he had said, 'I don't know where it's supposed to be.'

The bicycle was the only thing he took out with him; into the street. It was a few days before the car turned up again. Then he found it, two blocks away. This time it had two flat tyres and no one did anything about them. But a house down there was one of those with grass planted on the pavement outside and the garden-boy let him go back and forth once or twice with the petrol-motor mower. He went again next day and helped him. The garden-boy wanted to know if his father smoked and asked him to bring cigarettes. He said, 'My father's not here but when we're settled I'll ask for some for you.' He hardly ever went out now without meeting the old man somewhere; the old man seemed to expect him. He brought things out of his paper carrier and showed them to the boy, unwrapped them from rags and the advertising handouts that drift to city gutters. There was a tin finger, from a cigar, a torch without switch or glass, and a broken plastic duck: nothing like the funnel. But the old man, who had the lint of white hairs caught among the whorls on his head, spread the objects on the pavement with the confidence of giving pleasure and satisfaction. He took the boy's hand and put in it the base of some fancy box; this hand on the boy's was strong, shaky and cold, with thick nails the colour of the tortoise's shell in the old house. The box-base had held a perfume bottle and was covered with stained satin; to the boy it was a little throne but he didn't want it, it was a girl's thing. He said with an exaggerated shrug, 'No money.' 'Yes, my *baasie*, only shilling, shilling. The Lord bless you, *Nkosana*. Only shilling.'

The old man began to wrap it all up again; the base, the duck, the torch and the tin finger. Afterwards, the boy thought that next time he might take the tin finger for, say, two-and-a-half cents, or three. He'd have to buy something. As he rode back to the new house, there was the angle of a straw hat with a band in a little group chatting, accusing and laughing, and he called out, 'Hullo, my friend!'

'Yes, my friend!' the greeting came back, though the man didn't look round at him.

Then he thought he saw, without the white cap, the one who wanted to buy his watch, and with a hasty wobble of pleasurable panic he rode off fast down the hill, lifting

his hands from the bars a moment in case somebody was
looking, and taking a chance on the white Alsatian.

When she was not at the typewriter she was on her
knees for hours at a time, sorting out boxes and suitcases
of things to be got rid of. She had gone through the stuff
once when she packed up and left, setting aside hers from
his and being brought up short when she came upon some
of the few things that seemed indisputably theirs and
therefore neither to be disposed of nor rightfully claimed
by either. Now she went through all that was hers, and this
time, on a different principle of selection, set aside what was
useful, relevant and necessary from what was not. All the
old nest-papers went into the dustbin: letters, magazines,
membership cards, even photographs. Her knees hurt
when she rose but she sometimes went on again after she
and the child had eaten dinner, and he was in bed.

During the day she did not go out except for consulta-
tions with the lawyers and if Marguerite phoned at night to
hear the latest, she sat down at the telephone with a gin
and bitter lemon – the first opportunity she'd had to think
about herself even long enough to pour a drink. She had
spoken to no one round about and awareness of her surroundings was limited to annoyance latent in the repetition
of one worn, close-harmony record, mutedly blaring again
and again from nearby – a gramophone in some native's
khaya. But she was too busy getting straight to take much
notice of anything; the boy was getting a bit too much
freedom – still, he couldn't come to any harm, she supposed
he wouldn't go far away, while out of the way. She hadn't
seen any of the good friends, since she'd left, and that was
fine. There'd been altogether too much talk and everyone
ready to tell *her* what she ought to do, one day, and then
running off to discuss the 'other side of the story' the next –
naturally, it all got back to her.

Marguerite was quite right. She was simply going ahead
to provide a reasonable, decent life for herself and her child.

She had no vision of this life beyond the statement itself, constantly in her mind like a line of doggerel, and proclaimed aloud in the telephone conversations with Marguerite, but she was seized by the preoccupations of sorting out and throwing away, as if someone had said: dig here.

She walked round the house at night before she went to bed, and checked windows and doors. Of course, she was used to that; but when, as had so often happened, she was left alone in the other house, there were familiar servants who could be trusted. There was no one to depend on here; she had taken the first girl who came to the back door with a reference. It was December and the nights were beautiful, beautiful: she would notice, suddenly, while pulling in a window. Out there in the colour of moonstone nothing moved but the vibration of cicadas and the lights in the valley. Both seemed to make shimmering swells through the warm and palpable radiance. Out there, you would feel it on bare arms while you danced or talked, you could lie on your back on hard terrace stone and feel the strange vertigo of facing the stars.

It was a postcard of somewhere she had been, and had no power over her in the present. She went to bed and fell asleep at once as if in a night's lodging come upon in the dark.

But after the first few days something began to happen in the middle of the night. It happened every night, or almost every night (she was not sure; sometimes she might have dreamt it, or run, in the morning, the experience of two nights into one). Anyway, it happened often enough to make a pattern of the nights and establish, through unease, a sense of place that did not exist in the light of day.

It was natives, of course; simply one of the nuisances of this quiet neighbourhood. A woman came home in the early hours of the morning from some shebeen. Or she had no home and was wandering the streets. First she was on the edge of a dream, among those jumbled cries and voices where the lines of conscious and subconscious cross.

Then she drew closer and clearer as she approached the street, the house, the bed – to which the woman lying there was herself returning from sleep to wakefulness. There was the point at which the woman in the bed knew herself to be there, lying awake with her body a statue still in the attitude of sleep, and the shadowy room standing back all round her. She lay and listened to the shouts, singing, laughter and sudden cries. It was a monologue; there was no answer, no response. No one joined in the singing and the yells died away in the empty streets. It was impossible not to listen because, apart from the singing, the monologue was in English – always when natives were drunk or abusive they seemed to turn to English or Afrikaans; if it had been in their language she could have shut it out with a pillow over her ears, like the noise of cats. The voice lurched and rambled. Just when it seemed to be retreating, fading round a corner or down the hill, there would be a short, fearful, questioning scream, followed by a waiting silence: then there it was, coming back, very near now, so near that slithering footsteps and the loose slap of heels could be heard between the rise and fall of accusations, protests, and wheedling obscenities. '. . . telling L I A R S. I . . . you . . . don't say me I'm cunt . . . and telling liars . . . L-I-A-R-S . . .you know? you know ? . . . I'm love for that . . . LI-ARS . . . the man he want fuck . . . LI-A-A-RS . . . my darling I'm love . . . A H H-hahahahhahahOOOooee . . . YOU RUBBISH! YOU HEAR! YOU RUBBISH . . .'

And then slowly it was all gathered together again, it staggered away, the whole muddled, drunken burden of it dragged off somewhere, nowhere, anywhere it could not be heard any more. She lay awake until the streets had stifled and hidden it, and then she slept.

Until the next night.

The summons was out of the dark as if the voice came out of her own sleep like those words spoken aloud with which one wakes oneself with a start. YOU RUBBISH

... don't say me ... he want ... L-I-A-R-S ... don't say me.

Or the horrible jabber when a tape recorder is run backwards. Is that my voice? Shrill, ugly; merely back-to-front? L-I-A-R-S. The voice that had slipped the hold of control, good sense, self-respect, proper provision, the future to think of. My darling I'm love for that. AhhhhhhhahahhaOOoooeee. Laughing and snivelling; no answer; nobody there. No one. In the middle of the night, night after night, she forgot it was a native, a drunken black prostitute, one of those creatures with purple lips and a great backside in trousers who hung about after the men. She lay so that both ears were free to listen and she did not move or open her eyes on the outer dark.

Then one night the voice was right under her window. The dog next door was giving deep regular barks of the kind that a dog gives at a safe distance from uncertain prey, and between bouts of fisting on some shaky wooden door the voice was so near that she could hear breath drawn for each fresh assault. 'YOU HEAR? I tell you I'm come find ... YOU HEAR-R-R ... I'm come give you nice fuck ... YOU-OOO-HE-AAR?' The banging must be on the door of the servant's room of the next door house; the dividing wall between the two properties was not more than ten feet from her bedroom. No one opened the door and the voice grovelled and yelled and obscenely cajoled.

This time she got up and switched on the light and put on her dressing gown, as one does when there is a situation to be dealt with. She went to the window and leant out; half the sky was ribbed with cloud, like a beach in the moonlight, and the garden trees were thickly black – she could not see properly into the neighbour's over the creeper-covered wall, but she held her arms across her body and called ringingly, 'Stop that! D'you hear? Stop it at once!'

There was a moment's silence and then it all began again,

the dog punctuating the racket in a deep, shocked bay. Now lights went on in the neighbour's house and there was the rattle of the kitchen door being unbolted. A man in pyjamas was in her line of vision for a moment as he stood on the back step. 'Anything wrong?' The chivalrous, reassuring tone between equals of different sex.

'In your yard,' she called back. 'Some drunk woman's come in from the street.'

'Oh my God. Her again.'

He must have been barefoot. She did not hear anyone cross the yard but suddenly his voice bellowed, 'Go on, get out, get going ... I don't care what you've come for, just get on your feet and *hamba* out of my yard, go on, quickly, OUT!' 'No master, that boy he –' 'Get up!' 'Don't swear me –' There was a confusion of the two voices with his quick, hoarse, sober one prevailing, and then a grunt with a sharp gasp, as if someone had been kicked. She could see the curve of the drive through the spaced shapes of shrubs and she saw a native woman go down it, not one of the ladies in trousers but an ordinary servant, fat and middle-aged and drunk, in some garment still recognizably a uniform. 'All right over there?' the man called.

'Thanks. Perhaps one can get some sleep now.'

'You didn't send for the police?'

'No, no I hadn't done that.'

All was quiet. She heard him lock his door. The dog gave a single bark now and again, like a sob. She got into the cool bed and slept.

The child never woke during the night unless he was ill but he was always up long before any adult in the mornings. That morning he remembered immediately that he had left his bicycle out all night and went at once into the garden to fetch it. It was gone. He stared at the sodden long grass and looked wildly round from one spot to another. His mother had warned him not to leave anything outside

because the fence at the lower end of the garden, giving on
a lane, was broken in many places. He looked in the shed
although he knew he had not put the bicycle there. His
pyjamas were wet to the knees from the grass. He stuffed
them into the laundry basket in the bathroom and put on a
shirt and trousers. He went twice to the lavatory, waiting
for her to get up. But she was later than usual that morning,
and he was able to go into the kitchen and ask the girl for
his breakfast and eat it alone. He did not go out; quietly,
in his room, he began to unpack and set up the track for
his electric racing cars. He put together a balsawood glider
that somehow had never been assembled, and slipped off
to throw it about, with a natural air, down the end of the
garden where the bicycle had disappeared. From there he
was surprised to hear his mother's voice, not on the telephone but mingled with other voices in the light, high way
of grown-up people exchanging greetings. He was attracted
to the driveway; drawn to the figures of his mother, and a
man and woman dressed for town, pausing and talking, his
mother politely making a show of leading them to the house
without actually inviting them in. 'No, well, I was saying
to Ronald, it's all right if one's an old inhabitant, you
know –' the woman began, with a laugh, several times
without being allowed to finish. '– a bit funny, my asking
that about the police, but really, I can assure you –'
'Oh no, I appreciated –' '– assure you, they're as much
use as –' 'It *was*, five or six years ago, but it's simply become
a hang-out–' 'And the women! Those creatures in Allenby
Road! I was saying, one feels quite ashamed –' 'Well I
don't think I've had an unbroken night's sleep since I
moved in. That woman yelling down the street at two in
the morning.' 'I make a point of it – don't hang about my
property, I tell them. They're watching for you to go out at
night, that's the thing.' 'Every morning I pick up beer
cartons *inside* our wall, mind you –'

His mother had acknowledged the boy's presence, to
the others, by cupping her hand lightly round the back of

his head 'And my bicycle's been stolen,' he said, up into their talk and their faces.

'Darling – where?' His mother looked from him to the neighbours, presenting the sensation of a fresh piece of evidence. 'You see?' said the man. 'There you are!'

'Here, in the garden,' he said.

'There you are. Your own garden.'

'*That* you must report,' said the woman.

'Oh really – on top of everything else. Do I have to go myself, or could I phone, d'you think?'

'We'll be going past the police station on the hill, on our way to town. Ronald could just stop a minute,' the woman said.

'You give me the particulars and I'll do it for you.' He was a man with thick-soled, cherry-dark shoes, soaring long legs, an air force moustache and a funny little tooth that pressed on his lip when he smiled.

'What was the make, again – d'you remember?' his mother asked him. And to the neighbours, 'But please come inside – won't you have some coffee, quickly? I was just going to make myself – oh, it was a Raleigh, wasn't it? Or was that your old little one?' They went into the house, his mother explaining that she wasn't settled yet.

He told them the make, serial number, wheelbase and identifying dents of his bicycle. It was the first time he and his mother had had visitors in this house and there was quite a flurry to find the yellow coffee cups and something better than a plastic spoon. He ran in and out helping, and taking part in the conversation. Since they had only just got to know him and his mother, these people did not interrupt him all the time as the friends who came to the other house always had. 'And I bet I know who took it, too,' he said. 'There's an old native boy who just talks to anybody in the street. He's often seen me riding my bike down by the house where the white dog is.'

Nadine Gordimer

Abroad

Manie Swemmer talked for years about going up to Northern Rhodesia for a look around. His two boys, Thys and Willie, were there, and besides, he'd worked up there himself in the old days, the early thirties.

He knew the world a bit although he was born in Bontebokspruit. His grandmother had been a Scots woman, Agnes Swan, and there was a pack of relatives in Scotland; he hadn't got that far, but in a sergeants' mess in Alex just before Sidi Rezegh, when he was with the South African First Division, he had met a Douglas Swan who must have been a cousin – there was quite a resemblance about the eyes.

Yes, he thought of going up, when he could get away. He had been working for the Barends brothers, the last five years, he had put up the Volkskas Bank and the extensions to the mill as well as the new waiting rooms for Europeans and non-Europeans at the station. The town was going ahead. Before that, he worked for the Provincial Public Works Department, and had even had a spell in Pretoria, at the steel works. That was after the motor business went bust; when he came back from the war he had sold his share of the land to his uncle, and gone into the motor business with the money. Fortunately, as Manie Swemmer said to the people he had known all his life in the bar of Buks Jacobs' hotel on Saturdays after work, although he'd had no real training there wasn't much in the practical field he couldn't do. If he'd had certificates, he wouldn't have been working for a salary from Abel and Johnnie Barends today, that was for sure; but there you are. People still depended on him; if he wanted to take his car and drive up North, he needed three weeks, and who could Abel find to take his place and manage his gang of boys on the site?

He often said he'd like to drive up. It was a long way but he didn't mind the open road and he'd done it years ago when it was strip roads if you were lucky, and plain murder the rest of the way. His old '57 Studebaker would make it; he looked after her himself, and there were many people in the town – including Buks Jacobs from the hotel with his new Volkswagen combi – who wouldn't have anybody else touch their cars. Manie spent most of his Saturday afternoons under somebody's; he had no one at home (the boys' mother, born Helena Thys, had died of a diseased kidney leaving him to bring up the two little chaps all alone) and he did it more out of friendship than for anything else.

On Sundays, when he was always expected at the Gysbert Swemmers', he had remarked that he'd like to go up and have a look around. And there were his boys, of course. His cousin Gysbert said, 'Let them come down and visit you.' But they were busy making their way; Thys was on the mines, but didn't like it, Willie had left the brewery and was looking for an opening down in the capital. After the British Government gave the natives the country and the name was changed to Zambia, Gysbert said, 'Man, you don't want to go there now. What for? After you waited so long.'

But he had moved around the world a bit: Gysbert might run three hundred head of cattle, and was making a good thing out of tobacco and chillies as well as mealies on the old Swemmer farm where they had all grown up, but Gysbert had never been further than a holiday in Cape Town. Gysbert had not joined up during the war. Gysbert sat in their grandfather's chair at Sunday dinner and served roast mutton and sweet potatoes and rice to his wife and family, including Manie, and Gysbert's mother, Tante Adela. Tante Adela had her little plot on the farm where she grew cotton, and after lunch she sat in the dark *voorkamer*, beside the big radio and record player combination, and stuffed her cotton into the cushion-covers she cut from sheets of plastic foam. There was coffee on the stoep, handed round by pregnant daughters and daughters-in-law, and there were grandchildren whose mouths exploded huge bubbles of gum before Oom Manie and made him laugh. Gysbert even still drank *mampoer*, home-made peach brandy sent from the Cape, but Manie couldn't stand the stuff and never drank any spirits but Senator Brandy – Buks Jacobs, at the hotel, would set it up without asking.

At the end of the Sunday Manie Swemmer would drive home from the old family farm that was all Gysbert knew, past the fields shuffling and spreading a hand of mealies, then tobacco, and then chilli bushes blended by distance, like roof-tiles, into red-rose-yellows. Past the tractor and the thresher with its beard of torn husks, and down into the dip over the dried-up river bed, where they used to try and catch leguaans, as youngsters. Past the cattle nibbling among the thorn bushes and wild willow. Through the gates opened by picannins running with the kaffir dogs, from the kraal. Past the boys and their women squatting around paraffin tins of beer and pap, and the Indian store, old Y. S. Mia's, boarded up for Sunday, and all the hundred-and-one relations those people have, collected on the stoep of the bright pink house next to the store. At that time in the late afternoon the shadow of the hilly range had taken up the dam; Manie looked, always, for the glittering circles belched by fish. He fished there, in summer, still; the thorn trees they used to play under were dead, but stood around the water.

The town did not really leave the lands behind. His house in Pretorius Street was the same as the farm houses, a tin roof, a polished stoep on stumpy cement pillars darkening the rooms round two sides, paint the colour of the muddy river half-way up the outside walls and on the woodwork. Inside there was flowered linoleum and a sword-fern in a painted kaffir pot that rocked a little on its uneven base as he walked in. The dining table and six chairs he and Helena had bought when they got married, and Tante Adela's plastic foam cushions, covering the places on the sofa-back where the kids had bounced the springs almost through. He had a good old boy, Jeremiah, looking after him. The plot was quite big and was laid out in rows of beetroot, onions and cabbage behind a quince hedge. Jeremiah had his mealie patch down at his *khaya*. There were half-a-dozen Rhode Island Reds in the *hok*, and as for the tomatoes, half the town ate presents of Manie Swemmer's tomatoes.

He'd never really cleared out his sons' room, though once there'd been a young chappie from the railways looking for somewhere to rent. But Willie was only sixteen when he went up North to have a look round – that's how kids are, his brother Thys had gone up and it was natural – he might want to come back home again sometime. The beds were there, and Willie's collection of bottle-tops. On the netted-in stoep round the back there was his motorbike, minus wheels. Manie Swemmer often thought of writing to ask Willie what he ought to do with the bike; but the boys didn't answer letters often. In fact Willie was better than Thys; Thys hadn't written for about eighteen months, by the time the place had gone and changed its name from Northern Rhodesia to Zambia. Not that the change would frighten Manie Swemmer if he decided to make the trip. After all, it wasn't as if he were going to drag a woman up there. And it might be different for people with young daughters. But for someone like him, well, what did he have to worry about except himself ?

One September, when the new abbatoir was just about off his hands, he told the Barends brothers that he was taking leave. 'No, not down to Durban – I'm pushing off up there for a couple of weeks – ' His rising eyebrows and backward jerk of the head indicated the back of the hotel bar, the mountain range, the border.

'Gambia, Zambia! These fancy names. With the new kaffir government. Dr or Professor or whatever-he-calls-himself Kaunda,' said Carel Janse van Vuuren, the local solicitor, who had been articled in Johannesburg, making it clear by his amusement that he, too, knew something of the world.

'Tell your sons to come home here, man. *Hulle is onse mense.*' Dawie Mulder was hoping to be nominated as a candidate for the next provincial elections and liked to put a patriotic edge on his remarks.

'Oh they know their home, all right, don't you worry,' Manie Swemmer said, in English, because some of the regulars on the commercial travellers' run, old Joe Zeff and Edgar Bloch, two nice Jewish chappies, had set up the beers for the group. 'They'll settle down when they've had their fling, I'm not worried.'

'Up in this, uh, Northern Rhodesia – I heard the natives don't bother the white people on the mines, eh?' said Zeff. 'I mean you don't have to worry, they won't walk into your house or anything – after all, it's not a joke, you have a big kaffir coming and sitting down next to us here? It's all you're short of.'

Sampie Jacobs, the proprietor's wife and a business woman who could buy and sell any man in Bonteboksspruit, if it came to money matters, said, 'Willie was a bea-utiful child. When he was a little toddler! Eyes like saucers, and blue!' She hung the fly-swatter on its hook, and mentally catching somebody out, scratched at some fragment of food dried fast to a glass. 'If Helena could have seen him' – she reminded Manie Swemmer of the pimple-eroded youth who had bought an electric guitar on credit and gone away leaving his father to meet the instalments.

'They'll settle down! Thys is earning good money up there now, though, man. You couldn't earn money like that here! Not a youngster.'

'Twenty-six – no, twenty-seven by now,' said Sampie Jacobs.

'But Willie. Willie's not twenty-one.'

Buks Jacobs said, 'Well, you can have it for me, Oom Manie.'

'Man, I nearly died of malaria up there in thirty-two,' Manie Swemmer said, putting a fist on the counter. 'Good Lord, I knew the place when it was nothing but a railhead and a couple of mine shafts in the bush. There was an Irish doctor, that time, Fitzgerald was his name, he got my boss-boy to sponge me down every hour . . .'

On the third day of the journey, in the evening, the train drew into the capital, Lusaka. Manie Swemmer had taken the train, after all; it would have been different if there had been someone to drive up with him. But the train was more restful, and, with this trip in the back of his mind all the time, it was some years since he'd taken a holiday. He was alone in the second-class compartment until the Bechuanaland border, wondering if Abel Barends wouldn't make a mess, now, of that gang of boys it had taken years to get into shape, a decent gang of boys but they had to know where they were with you, the native doesn't like to be messed around, either. He mouthed aloud to himself what he had meant to say to Abel, 'Don't let me come back and find you've taken on a lot of black scum from the location.' But then the train stopped at a small station and he got up to lean on the let-down window; and slowly the last villages of the Transvaal were paused at and passed, and as he looked out at them with his pipe in his mouth and the steam letting fly from beneath the carriage, Barends and the building gang sank to the bottom of his mind. Once or twice, when the train moved on again, he checked his post office savings book (he had transferred money to Lusaka) and the indigestion pills he had put in with his shaving things. He had his bedding ticket (Everything under control, he had joked, smiling to show how easy it was if you knew

how, to Gysbert and his wife and Sampie Jacobs, who had
seen him on to the train) and a respectful coloured boy made
up a nice bunk for him and was grateful for his five cent tip.
By the time the train reached Mafeking after dinner, he
felt something from the past that he had forgotten entirely,
although he talked about it often: the jubilant lightness of
moving on, not a stranger among strangers, but a new
person discovered among new faces. He felt as if he had been
travelling for ever and could go on for ever. The hills, the
bush, the smell of a certain shrub came back to him across
thirty years. It was like the veld at home, only different. The
balancing rocks, the white-barked figs that split them and
held them in tightspread roots, the flat-topped trees turning
red with spring – yes, he remembered that – the bush
becoming tangled forest down over the rivers, the old
baobabs and the kaffir-orange trees with their green
billiard-balls sticking out all over, the huge vleis with, far
off, a couple of palms craning up looking at you. Two more
days slid past the windows. He bought a set of table mats
from a picannin at a siding; nicely made, the reeds dyed
pink and black – he saw Sampie Jacobs putting them under
her flower arrangements in the hotel lounge, far, far away
far, far ahead. When the train reached the Rhodesian-
Zambian border there was a slight nervous bracing of his
manner: he laid out his open passport – HERMANUS
STEFANUS SWEMMER, national of the Republic of
South Africa. The young Englishman and the black man
dressed exactly like him, white socks, gold shoulder tabs,
smart cap, the lot, said, 'Thank you sir'; the black one
scribbled and stamped.

Well, he was in.

As the train neared Lusaka he began to get anxious.
About Willie. About what he would say to Willie. After all,
five years. Willie's twenty-first was coming up in December.
He forgot that he was drawing into Lusaka through the dark,
he forgot that he was travelling, he thought: Willie, Willie.
There were no outskirts to Lusaka, even now. A few lights

at a level crossing or two, bicycles, native women with bundles – and they were in the station. The huge black sky let down a trail of rough bright stars as close as the lights of a city. Bells rang and the train, standing behind Manie Swemmer, stamped backwards. People sauntered and yelled past him: white people, Indians, natives in moulded plastic shoes.

Willie said, 'Hell, where were you?'

Tall. Sideburns. A black leather jacket zipped up to where the button was missing at the neck of the shirt. The same; and Manie Swemmer had forgotten. Never sent a snap of himself, and naturally you'd expect him to have changed in five years.

They spoke in English. 'I was just beginning to wonder did the letter get lost. I was just going to take a taxi. Well, how's it! Quite a trip, eh? Since Wednesday, man!' Manie knew how to behave; he had his hands on the kid's biceps, he was pushing him and shaking him. Willie was grinning down the side of his mouth. He stood there while his father talked about the train, and why he hadn't driven up, and what Gysbert said, that backvelder tied to Tante Adela's apron, and the good dinner the dining car had put up. 'Give us your things,' Willie said. 'What's this?' The mats were tied up in a bit of newspaper. 'Presents, man. I can't go back empty-handed.' 'Just hang on here a minute, ay, Dad, I'mna get some smokes.' Held his shoulders too high when he ran; that was always his fault, when he did athletics at Bontebokspruit High. Willie. Couldn't believe it. Suddenly Manie Swemmer landed in Lusaka, knew he was there, and exhilaration spread through his breast like some pleasurable form of heartburn.

Willie opened the pack and shook out a cigarette, tenting his hands round the match. 'Where were you gunna take the taxi?'

'Straight to your place, man. I've got the letter on me.'

'I've pushed off from there.'

'But what happened, son, I thought it was so near for work and everything?'

Willie took a deep draw at his cigarette, put his head back as if swallowing an injury and then blew smoke at it, with narrowed eyes; there was a line between them, already, his father noticed. 'Didn't work out at Twyford's Electric. So I had to find a cheaper room until I get fixed up.'

'But I thought they told you there was prospects, son?'

'I'm going to see someone at the cement works Monday. Friend of mine says he'll fix me up. And there's a job going at a motor spares firm, too. I don't want to jump at anything.'

'For Pete's sake, no. You must think of your future. Fancy about Twyford's, eh, they started up in the thirties, one of the first. But I suppose the old boy's dead now. Watch out for the motor spares outfit – I don't trust that game.'

They were still standing on the platform; Willie was leaning against one of the struts that held up the roof, smoking and feeling a place near his left sideburn where he had nicked himself. That poor kid would never be able to get a clean shave – his skin had never come right. He seemed to have forgotten about the luggage.

'So where you staying now, Willie?' Everyone from the train had left.

'I'm at another chap's place. There's a bed on the stoep. There's five people in the house, only three rooms. They can't put you up.'

'What's wrong with a hotel?' Manie Swemmer consoled, chivvying, cheerful. 'Come let's take this lot and get into town. I'll get a room at the Lusaka Hotel, good Lord, do I remember that place. I know all about the posh new one out on the Ridgeway, too. But I don't have to splash it. The Lusaka'll do me fine.'

Willie was shaking his head, hang-dog.

'You'll never get in, man, Dad. You don't know – you won't get a room in this place. It's the independence anniversary next week –'

'When? The anniversary, eh – ' He was pleased to have arrived for a festival.

'I dunno. Monday. I think. You haven't a hope.'

'Wait a minute, wait a minute.' They were gathering the luggage, Manie Swemmer had put on his hat to emerge into the town, although he had suddenly realized that the night was very hot. He looked at his son.

'I thought maybe it's the best thing if you go straight on to the Copper Belt,' said Willie. 'To Thys.'

'To Thys?' He lifted the hat to let the air in upon his head.

'I dunno about a train, but it's easy to thumb a lift on the road.'

'The Regent!' Manie Swemmer said. 'Is there still a Regent Hotel? Did you try there?'

'What you mean try, Dad, I told you, it's no use to *try*, you'll never get *in* –'

'Well, never mind, son, let's go and have a beer there, anyway. Okay?' Manie Swemmer felt confused, as if the station itself were throwing back and forth all sorts of echoes. He wanted to get out of it, never mind where. There was only one clear thought; silly. He must put new buttons on the kid's shirt. A man who has brought up two youngsters and lived alone a long time secretly knows how to do these things.

Lusaka was a row of Indian stores and the railway station, facing each other. In the old days.

Manie Swemmer was a heavy man but he sat delicately balanced, forward, in the taxi, looking out under the roof at the new public buildings and shopping centres lit up round paved courts in Cairo Road, the lights of cars travelling over supermarkets and milk bars. 'The post office? Ne-ver!' And he could not stop marvelling at it, all steel and glass, and a wide parking lot paved beside it. Here and there was a dim landmark – one of the Indian stores whose cracked verandah had been a quay above the dust of the road – with a new shopfront but the old tin roof. No more sewing machines going under the hands of the old natives on the verandahs; even just in passing, you could see the stuff in the smart window displays was factory-made. Fishing tackle and golf clubs; shiny sets of drums and electric guitars; a grubby-looking little bar with kaffir music coming out. 'Looks as if it should be down in the location, eh?' He laughed, pointing it out to Willie. There were quite a few nicely-dressed natives about, behaving themselves, with white shirts and ties. The women in bright cotton dresses, the latest styles, and high-heeled shoes. And everywhere, Europeans in cars. 'Ah, but the old trees are still going strong!' he said to Willie. Along the middle of the Cairo Road there was the same broad island with red-flowering trees, he recognized the shape of the blooms although he couldn't see their colour. Willie was sitting back, smoking. He said, 'They don't leave you alone, with their potatoes and I don' know what.' He wasn't looking, but was speaking of the natives who hung around even after dark under the trees – vendors, young out-of-works.

The way to the Regent was too short for Manie Swemmer's liking. He could have done with driving around a bit; this kind of confusion was different – exciting, like being blind-folded, whirled around, and then left to feel your way about a room you knew well. But in no time they were at the hotel, and that had changed and hadn't changed, too. The old rows of rooms in the garden had been connected with a new main building, but the 'garden' was still swept earth with a few hibiscus and snake plants.

They found themselves in what had been the verandah and was closed in with glass louvres and called the terrace lounge. Willie made no suggestions, and his father, chatting and commenting in the husky undertone he used among other people, was misled by the layout of the hotel as he remembered it. 'Never mind, never mind! What's the odds. We'll have a drink before we start any talking, man, why not? This'll do all right,' and with his big behind in its neat grey flannels rising apologetically towards the room, he supervised the stowing of his two suitcases and news-paper parcel beside the small table where he urged Willie to sit. He ordered a couple of beers, and looked around. The place was filling up with the sort of crowd you get on hot evenings; one or two families with kids climbing about the chairs, young men buying their girls a drink, married couples who hadn't gone home after the office – men alone would be in the pub itself. There was only one coloured couple – not blacks, more like Cape Coloureds. You'd hardly notice them. Willie didn't know anyone. They went, once again, over the questions and answers they had exchanged over Willie's prospects of a new job. But it had always been hard to know what Willie was thinking, even when he was quite a little kid; and Manie Swemmer's attention kept getting out of range, around the room, to the bursts of noise that kept coming, perhaps when some inner door connected with the bar was opened – to the strange familiar town outside, and the million and one bugs going full blast for the night with the sound of sizzling, of clocks being wound, and ratchets jerking. 'What a machine shop, eh?' he said; but of course, living there five years, Willie wouldn't even be hearing it anymore.

'Who's running the place these days?' he suggested to Willie confidentially, when the beer was drunk. 'You know the chap at all?'

'Well, I mean I know who he is. Mr Davidson. We come here sometimes. There's a dance, first Saturday of the month.'

'Do you think he'd know you?'

'I don't know if he knows me,' said Willie.

'Well, come on, let's see what we can do.' Manie Swem-mer asked the Indian waiter to keep an eye on the luggage for a moment, and was directed to the reception desk. Willie came along behind him. A redhead with a skin that would dent blue if you touched it said, 'Full up, sir, I'm sorry, sir – ' almost before Manie Swemmer began speaking. He put his big, half-open fist on the counter, and smiled at her with his head cocked: 'Now listen here, young miss, I come all the way from a place you never heard of, Bontebokspruit, and I'm sure you can find me just a bed. Anywhere. I've travelled a lot and I'm not fussy.' She smiled sympathetically, but there it was – nothing to offer. She even ran her ballpoint down the list of bookings once again, eyebrows lifted and the pretty beginnings of a double chin showing.

'Look, I lived in this town while you were still a twinkle in your father's eye – I'd like to say hello to Mr Davidson, anyway. D'you mind, eh?' She called somewhere behind a stand of artificial roses and tulips, 'Friend of Mr Davidson's here. Can he come a minute?'

He was a little fellow with a recognizable way of hitching his arms forward at the elbow to ease his shirt cuffs up his wrists as he approached: ex-barman. He had a neat, patient face, used to dealing with trouble.

'Youngster like you wouldn't remember, but I lived in this hotel thirty years ago – I helped build this town, put up the first reservoir. Now they tell me I'll have to sleep in the street tonight.'

'That's about it,' the manager said.

'I can hear you're a Jock, like me, too!' Manie Swemmer seized delightedly upon the hint of a Scots accent. 'Yes, you may not believe it but my grandmother was a Miss Swan. From the Clyde. Agnes Swan. I used to wear the kilt when I was a kiddie. Yes, I did! An old Boer like me.'

The little man and the receptionist conferred over the list of bookings; she knew she was right, there was nothing. But the man said, 'Tell you what I'll do. There's this fellow from Delhi. He's a biggish single I could m'be put another bed in. I promised him he'd have it to himself, but still an' all. He can't object to someone like yourself, I mean.'

'There you are! The good old Regent! Didn't I say to you, Willie?' Willie was leaning on the reception desk smoking and looking dazedly at the high heel of his Chelsea boot; he smiled down the side of his mouth again.

'I'll apologize for barging in on this chap, don't you worry, I'll make it all right. You say from Delhi – India?' Manie Swemmer added suddenly. 'You mean an Indian chappie?'

'But he's not one of your locals,' said the manager. 'Not one of these fellows down here. A businessman, flown in this morning on the V.C.10.'

'Oh, he's well-dressed, a real gentleman,' the receptionist reassured in the wide-eyed recommendation of something she wouldn't care to try for herself.

'That's the way it is,' the manager said, in confidence.

'O.K., O.K., I'll buy. I'm not saying a word!' said Manie Swemmer. 'Ay, Willie? Somewhere to lay my head, that's all I ask.'

The redhead took a key out of the nesting boxes numbered on the wall. 'Fifty-four, Mr Davidson? The boy'll bring your luggage, sir.'

'Good Lord, you've got to have a bit of a nerve or you don't get anywhere, eh?' Manie walked gaily close beside his son along the corridors with their path of flowered runner and buckets of sand filled with cigarette stubs, stepping round beer bottles and tea-trays that people had put outside their doors. In the room that the servant opened for him, he at once assumed snug possession. 'I hope the oriental gentleman's only going to stay one night. This'll do me fine.' A divan, ready made-up with bedding and folded in the middle like a wallet was wheeled in. He squeaked cupboards open, forced up the screeching steel flyscreens and pushed the windows wide – 'Air, air, that's what we need.' Willie sat on the other bed, whose cover had already been neatly turned back to allow a head to rest on the pillow; the dent was still there. The chap's things were on the dressing table. Willie fingered a pair of cufflinks with red stones in them. There was a tissue-paper airmail edition of some London newspaper, an open tin of cough lozenges, and a gold-tooled leather notebook. Rows of exquisitely neat figures, and then writing like something off a fancy carpet: 'Hell, look at this, eh?' said Willie.

'Willie, I always taught you to respect other people's belongings no matter who they are.'

Willie dropped the notebook finickily. 'Okay, okay.'

Manie Swemmer washed, combed his moustache and the back of his head, where there was still some hair, put back on again the tropical-weight jacket he had bought especially for the trip. 'I never used to look sloppy, not even when the heat was at its height,' he remarked to Willie. Willie nodded whether he had been listening to what you said or not.

When they had returned the key to the reception desk Willie said, 'We gunna eat now, Dad,' but there wasn't a soul in the dining room but a young woman finishing supper with her kiddies, and if there was one thing that depressed Manie Swemmer it was an empty hotel dining room.

In fact, he was attracted to the bar with a mixture of curiosity and shyness, as if Manie Swemmer, twenty-three years old, in bush-jacket and well-pressed shorts, might be found drinking there. He strolled through the garden, Willie behind him, listening to the tree-frogs chinking away at the night. In spite of the town, you could still smell woodsmoke from the natives' fires. But youngsters don't notice these things. The street entrance to the bar was through a beer garden, now screened by lattice. Coloured bulbs poked red and blue light through the pattern of slats and dark blotches of creeper. There were loud voices in the local native lingo and the coughs of small children. 'It's for them, let's go this way,' Willie said, and he and his father went back into the hotel and entered the bar from the inside door.

It was full all right. Manie Swemmer had never been what you would call a drinker, but for a man who lives alone there is no place where he feels at home the way he does among men in a bar. And yet there were blacks. Oh yes, that was something. Blacks sitting at the tables, and some of them not too clean or well-dressed either. Looked like boys from the roads, labourers. Up at the bar were the white men, the wide backs and red necks almost solidly together; a black face or two above white shirts at the far end. The backs parted for father and son: they might have been expected. 'Well, what's the latest from Thys, man?' Manie Swemmer was at ease at last, wedged between the shoulder of a man telling a story with large gestures and the bar counter ringed shinily, like the dark water at Gysbert's dam.

'Nothing. Oh this girl. He's got himself engaged to this doll Lynda Thompson.'

'Good grief, so he must have written! The letter's missed me. Getting engaged! Well, I've picked the right time, eh, independence anniversary and my son's engagement! We've got something to drink to, all right. When's the engagement going to be?'

'Oh it was about ten days ago. A party at her people's place in Kitwe. I couldn't get a lift up to the Copper Belt that weekend.'

'But if I'd known! Why'n't Thys send me a telegram, man! I'd have taken my leave sooner!'

Willie said nothing, only looked sideways at the men beside him.

Manie Swemmer took a deep drink of his beer. 'If he'd sent a telegram, man! Why'n't he let me know? I told him I was coming up the middle of the month. Why not just send a telegram at least?'

Willie had no answer. Manie Swemmer drank off his beer and ordered another round. Now he said softly, in Afrikaans, 'Just go to the post office and write out a telegram, eh?'

Willie shrugged. They drank. The swell of other people's spirits, the talk and laughter around them lifted Manie Swemmer from the private place where he was beached. 'Well, I'll go up and look at Miss Lynda Thompson for myself in a few days. Kitwe's a beautiful town, eh? What's the matter with the girl, is he ashamed of her or what?

Is she bowlegged and squints?' He laughed. 'Trust old Thys for that!'

At some point the shoulder pressing against his had gone without his noticing. A native's voice said in good English, 'Excuse me, did you lose this?' The black hand with one of those expensive calendar watches at the wrist held out a South African two rand note.

Manie Swemmer began struggling to get at his pockets. 'Hang on a tick, just let me . . . yes, must be mine, I pulled it out by mistake to pay with . . . thanks very much.'

'A pleasure.'

One of the educated kind, some of them have studied at universities in America even. And England was just pouring money into the hands of these people, they could go over and get the best education going, better than whites could afford. Manie Swemmer said to Willie, but in a voice to be overheard, because after all, you didn't expect such honesty of a native, it was really something to be encouraged: 'I thought I'd put away all my money from home when I took out my Zambian currency in the train. Two rand! Well, that would have been the price of a few beers down the drain!'

The black said, 'The price of a good bottle of brandy down there.' He wore a spotless bush jacket and longs; spotless.

'You've been to South Africa?' said Manie Swemmer.

'You ever heard of Fort Hare College? I was there four years. And I used to spend my holidays with some people in Germiston. I know Johannesburg well.'

'Well, let me buy you a South African brandy. Come on, man, why not?' The black man smiled and indicated casually that his bottle of beer had already been put before him. 'No, no, man, that'll do for a chaser; you're going to have a brandy with me, eh?' Manie Swemmer's big body curved over the bar as he agitated for the attention of the barman. He jolted the black man's arm and almost threw Willie's glass over. 'Sorry – come on, there – two brandies – wait a minute, have you got Senator? D'you want another beer, Willie?' The kid might drink brandy on his own but he wasn't going to get it from his father.

'You'll get a shock when you have to pay.' The black chap was amused. He had taken a newspaper out of his briefcase and was glancing over the headlines.

'Brandy's expensive here, eh? The duty and that. When I was up on the Copper Belt as a youngster we had to drink it to keep going. Brandy and quinine. It was a few bob a bottle. That's how I learnt to drink brandy.'

'Is that so?' The black man spoke kindly. 'So you know this country quite a long time.'

Manie Swemmer moved his elbow within half-an-inch of a nudge – 'I'll bet I knew it before you did – before you were born!'

'I'm sure, I'm sure.' They laughed. Manie Swemmer looked excitedly from the man to his son, but Willie was mooning over his beer, as usual. The black man – he told his name but who could catch their names – was something in the Ministry of Local Government, and he was very interested in what Manie Swemmer could tell him of the old days; he listened with those continual nods of the chin that showed he was following carefully; a proper respect – if not for a white man, then for a man as old as his father might be. He could still speak Afrikaans, Manie Swemmer discovered. He said a few sentences in a low voice but Manie Swemmer was pretty sure he could have carried on a whole conversation if he'd wanted to. 'You'll excuse me if I don't join you, but you'll have another brandy?' the black man offered. 'I have a meeting in' – he looked at the watch – 'less than half-an-hour, and I must keep a clear head.'

'Of course! You've got responsibility now. I always say, any fool can learn to do what he's told, but when it comes to making the decisions, when you got to shift for yourself, that's the time you've either got it up here, or. . . . It doesn't matter who or what you are . . .'

The man had slipped off the bar stool, briefcase between chest and arm. 'Enjoy your holiday . . .'

'Everything of the best!' Manie Swemmer called after him. 'I'll tell you something, Willie, he may be black as the ace of spades, but that's a gentleman. Eh? You got to be open-minded, otherwise you can't move about in these countries. But that's a gentleman!'

'Some of them put on an act,' said Willie. 'You get them wanting to show how educated they are. The best thing is don't take any notice.'

'What's the name of that feller was talking to me?' Manie Swemmer asked the white barman. He wanted to write it down so he'd be able to remember when he told the story back home.

'You know who that is? That's Thompson Gwebo, that's one of the Under Minister's brothers,' the barman said. 'When he married last November they had their roast oxen and all that at his village, but the wedding reception for the government people and white people and so on was here. Five tiers to the cake. Over three hundred people. Mrs Davidson did the snacks herself.'

They began to chat, between interruptions when the barman was called away to dispense drinks. Two or three beers had their effect on Willie, too; he was beginning to talk, in reluctant spates that started with one of his mumbled remarks, half-understood by his father, and then developed, through his father's eager questions, into the bits and pieces of a life that Manie Swemmer pieced together. 'This feller said ...' 'Which one was that, the manager or your mate?' 'No, the one I told you ... the one who was supposed to turn up at the track ...' 'What track?' 'Stock car racing ... there was this feller asked me to change the plugs ...'

In a way, it was just like the old days up there. Nobody thought about going home. Not like Buks Jacobs' place, the pub empty over dinner-time. This one was packed. The white men were solid at the bar again, but the blacks at the tables – the labourers – were getting rowdy. They were joined by a crowd of black ducktails in jeans who behaved

just like the white ones you saw in the streets of Johannesburg and Pretoria. They surged up and down between the
tables and were angrily hit off, like flies, by the labourers
heavily drunk over their beer: one lifted his bottle and
brought it down on the back of one of the hooligans' hands;
there was a roar. A black lout in a shirt with 007 printed
across it kept stepping back against Manie Swemmer's
back in the brand-new tropical jacket. Manie Swemmer
went on talking and ignored him, but the hooligan taunted
in English – 'Sorry!' He did it again: 'Sorry!' The drunken
black face with a fleck of white matter at the corner of each
eye breathed over him. If it'd been a white man Manie
Swemmer wouldn't have stood for it, he'd have punched
him in the nose. And at home if a native – but at home it
couldn't happen; here he was, come up to have a look, and
he'd been in some tough spots before – Good Lord, those
gyppos in Egypt, they didn't all smell of roses, either. He
knew how to hold himself in if he had to.

Then another native – one in a decent shirt and tie –
came over and said something angrily, in their own language, to the hooligans. He said to the barman in English,
'Can't you see these men are making a nuisance of themselves? Why don't you have them thrown out?'

The barman was quick to take the support. 'These people
should be outside in the beer garden!' he said to the company at large. 'Go on, I don't want trouble in here.' The
hooligans drifted away from the bar counter but would not
go out. Manie Swemmer had not noticed the decently
dressed native leave, but suddenly he appeared, quiet and
businesslike, with two black policemen in white gloves.
'What's the complaint?' One shouldered past Willie to ask
the barman. 'Making a nuisance of themselves, those over
there.' There was a brief uproar; of course natives are great
ones for shouting. But the black hooligans were carted away
by their own policemen like a bunch of scruffy dogs; no
nonsense.

'No nonsense!' said Manie Swemmer, laughing and

putting his hand over Willie's forearm. 'D'you see that? Good Lord, they've got marvellous physiques, that pair. Talk about smart! That's something worth seeing!' Willie giggled; his Dad was talking very loud; he was talking to everyone in the place, joking with everyone. At last they found themselves at dinner, after half-past nine it must have been. There were shouts of laughter from other late diners telling stories. Manie Swemmer began to think very clearly and seriously, and to talk very seriously to Willie about the possibility of moving up here himself. 'I've still got a lot of my life ahead of me. Must I see out my time making money for Abel Barends? In Bontebokspruit? Why shouldn't I start out on my own again? The place is going ahead!'

The jolly party left the dining room and all at once he was terribly tired: the journey, the arrival, the first look around – it left him winded, like too hearty a slap on the back. 'Let's call it a day, son,' he said, and Willie saw him to the room.

But the key would not open the door. Willie investigated by the flare of a match. 'S'bolted on the inside.' They rapped softly, then hammered. 'Well I'm damned,' said Manie Swemmer. 'The Indian.' He had been going to tell him about how many years Y. S. Mia had had a store near the farm.

They went down to the reception desk. The redhead thrust her tongue in a bulge between lower lip and teeth, in consternation. 'Have you knocked?' 'The blooming door down!' said Manie Swemmer. 'Mind you, I thought as much,' the girl said. 'He was on his high horse when he came back and saw your bed and things. I mean I don't know what the fuss was about – as I said to him, it isn't as if we've put an African in with you, it's a white man. And him Indian himself.'

'Well, what're you going to do about my Dad?' Willie said suddenly.

'What can I do?' She made a peaked face. 'Mr Davidson's gone off to Kapiri Mposhi, his mother's broken her hip at eighty-one. I can't depend on anyone else here to throw that chap out. And if he won't even answer the door.'

Manie Swemmer said nothing. Willie waited, but all he could hear was his father's slow breathing, with little gasps on the intake. 'But what about my Dad?'

She had her booking list out again. They waited. 'Tell you what. No. – There's a room with four beds out in the old wing, we keep it, you know – sometimes now, these people come in and you daren't say no. They don't want to pay for more than one room for the lot. It was booked, I mean, but it's after eleven now and no one's showed up, so I should think you could count on it being all right . . .'

Manie Swemmer put his big forearm and curled hand on the reception desk like a dead thing. 'Look,' he said. 'The coolie, all right, I didn't say anything. But don't put me in with an African, now, man! I mean, I've only just got here, give me a bit of time. You can't expect to put me in with a native, right away, first thing.'

'Oh I should think it would be all right,' she said in her soothing, effusive way, something to do with some English accent she had. 'I wouldn't worry if I was you. It's late now. Very unlikely anyone'd turn up. Don't you think?'

She directed him to the room. Willie went with him again. Across the garden; the old block, the way it was in the old days. There was no carpet in the passage; their footsteps tottered over the unevennesses of cracked granolithic. When Willie had left him, he pulled down the bedding of the best-looking bed to have a good look at the sheets, opened the window, and then, working away at it with a grunt that was almost a giggle, managed to drive the rusty bolt home across the door.

Shiva Naipaul

A Man of Mystery

Grant Street could boast several business establishments: a grocery, a bookshop that sold chiefly Classic comics, a café and, if you were sufficiently enthusiastic, the rum-shop around the corner (known as the Pax Bar) could also be included. On week-ends a coconut seller arrived with his donkey cart which he parked on the corner. The street's commercial character had developed swiftly but with the full approval of its residents. Commerce attracted strangers and the unbroken stream of traffic lent an air of excitement and was a source of pride. In time a group of steelbandsmen had established themselves in one of the yards, adding thereby a certain finality and roundness to the physiognomy of the street. However, long before any of these things had happened, Grant Street could point to Mr Edwin Green, 'shoemaker and shoe-repairer', whose workshop had been, until the recent immigrations, the chief landmark and point of reference.

From the first Mr Green had been considered by his neighbours to be different from themselves. There were good reasons for this. Grant Street lived an outdoor, communal life. Privacy was unknown and if anyone had demanded it he would have been laughed at. There were good reasons for this as well. The constant lack of privacy had led ultimately to a kind of fuzziness with regard to private property. No one was sure, or could be sure, what belonged to whom or who belonged to whom. When this involved material objects, like bicycles, there would be a fight. When it involved children, more numerous on Grant Street than bicycles, there was a feckless tolerance of the inevitable doubts about paternity. Young men in pursuit of virility made false claims, while at other times the true father absconded. No one worried, since in any case the child would eventually be absorbed into the life of the street. Romantic relationships, frankly promiscuous, were fleeting rather than fragile, and the influx of strangers accelerated this tendency. Unfortunately, the results then were less happy. Grant Street was communal, but only up to a point, and any attachment one of its women might develop for a man from another street was looked upon with distaste. The inevitable child became the centre of a feud. Paternity in the stricter sense was of course not the issue. To which street did the child belong? It was over this problem that argument and acrimony raged.

Mr Green had been deposited in their midst like an alien body. Not only was he married, but his wife, a woman of half-Portuguese, half-Negro extraction, was pale-complexioned, good-looking and 'cultured'. In the late afternoon when Mr Green had closed his shop for the day, she would bring an easel out into the yard and paint for an hour. She had a fondness for sailing ships sinking in stormy seas and vases of flowers. The street, to begin with, had gathered solemnly around her and watched. She enjoyed their bewilderment.

'Lady, why you does paint when it so dark for?'

Mrs Green would stare seriously at her questioner.

'It's the light. There's a certain quality to this tropical twilight which I find so ... so exhilarating.'

Her accent was 'foreign' and when she spoke her bosom heaved cinematically, suggesting a suppressed passion. This impressed her audience. Mrs Green also frequented the public library. On Saturday mornings the street saw her struggling under the weight of half a dozen books, the titles of which were conspicuously displayed. The women sitting on their front steps would laugh in awed disbelief and shout after her, 'Soon you go read up all the books they have in the library. You go have to begin writing them yourself then.' Mrs Green, looking martyred, would disappear into her yard.

All of this was curious enough, but what really intrigued the street was her attitude to Mr Green. They could not understand it. They were never seen together. During the day while he hammered in his shop, she was nowhere in evidence, while during her afternoon painting sessions, he in his turn seemed to have been swallowed up by the silence in their house. That silence was another cause for speculation. It was an unnatural, abnormal silence which many believed to be in some strange way a counterpart to the suppressed passion they thought they detected in Mrs Green's voice.

Nevertheless it was on her husband that the street's perplexity and wonder finally came to rest. The incongruities were not hard to find. Mr Green was spectacularly black, he was ugly, and he betrayed none of the outward signs of culture which his wife exhibited. Stated so baldly the problem was insoluble. That could not be tolerated. Therefore, the belief took shape that Mr Green was something other than he appeared to be. He was not a shoemaker at all; on the contrary, he was a man of the highest education who had chosen that lowly profession out of a profound and philosophic love for the 'simple life'. Mr Green, it was claimed, was in revolt against the hypocrisy and useless trappings of modern civilization. Also for a time it was fashionable to uphold the theory that Mr Green spent much of his time in a trance, but that was soon abandoned as being too improbable. Nevertheless it did not hinder his transformation into a man of mystery.

His shop became the centre of romance for children on the street. It was a small wooden hut situated at the front of the house (itself an enlarged hut on stilts) under the shade of a tall tamarind tree. Above the door there was a sign which claimed he had the ability 'to fit all sizes and conform to all tastes'. This was a piece of rhetoric. As far as anyone could tell, Mr Green had not once been commissioned to make a pair of shoes; he simply repaired them. Inside there was a clutter of old, unreclaimed shoes overspread with dust. On a sagging work-table he arranged those recently brought in for repair and, always in the same place, an American trade magazine for the year 1950. Mr Green worked facing away from the light. He sat on a bench, holding several tiny nails between his teeth, occasionally extracting one which he would tack with exaggerated care into the shoe he was holding. After each such operation he examined the shoe from all angles and shook his head mournfully. The children crowding near him savoured the smells of leather in various stages of decomposition and the bottles of glue which lay open beside him.

Gradually from his conversations with the children a picture of his past was pieced together. He had lived in Brazil for many years where he had worked as a tapper on a rubber plantation. There he had met his wife, the daughter of the overseer, a hard and unfeeling man who kept his daughter a virtual prisoner and beat her regularly and viciously. She had begged him to take her away – he was the only foreigner working on the plantation – and together they had fled to British Guiana where she had borne him a child, a daughter. They had named her Rosa. The overseer having by that time repented, and they being extremely poor, the child was sent back to Brazil to live with her grandfather. In the meantime, they had saved sufficient money to buy a house and it was thus they had come to Trinidad and to Grant Street. His one sadness in life was never to have seen his daughter – 'a full and grown woman now' – and it was only the hope of seeing her again that kept him 'alive'.

This was a far cry from the picture that had been built up, and while no one really believed the story, it did have its attractions. Therefore the street pretended to believe that it believed Mr Green. He made their task easy. He was everything they expected him to be: kind, gentle, and a little sad. His eccentricities pleased them, especially his dress for occasions, which was invariable and immaculate. He wore a starched and ironed white tropical suit and a cork hat, and when he began taking the children for walks the men lounging on the corner murmured as he passed them, 'Make way for the Governor, everybody make way for the Governor.'

On his Sunday walks Mr Green took the children to the zoo and botanical gardens. They went early in the afternoon, marching in military formation behind Mr Green, who walked stiffly ahead of them. When they had come to the highest point in the Queen's Park Savannah, he would gather the children more informally about him and show them the sea and the ships in the harbour. 'The Brazils,' he would say, 'lie in that direction, and Venezuela, which from certain points you can see on a clear day, in that.' His arms extended in a sweep that embraced the harbour and the glittering sea beyond. When this ritual had been performed, they crossed the road to the zoo. He appeared to have a taste only for those animals he had seen in the wild. 'They call those jaguars? Who they trying to fool? I'll tell you about a jaguar I saw in Brazil one time.' And he would relate a long and tortuous tale. The birds, though, were his favourites and he was at his most lyrical when talking about them. 'They call those parrots? I've seen them in the wild. The colours of the rainbow and more besides. Wonderful creatures. They belong in the jungle,' and adjusting his hat he led them to the alligator pond, as if what he had just seen had been calculated to offend him personally.

Afterwards, they went to the botanical gardens, which, at six o'clock, would be nearly empty. There he allowed them to rest, and while they sprawled on the grass he wandered along the gravelled paths, staring up at the trees, occasionally bending close to read the labels attached to the trunks. Sometimes, perhaps struck by the sudden recall of an incident or a landscape long forgotten, he left off his examination of the trees and gazed abstractedly at the flag flapping limply above the roof of the Governor's house, itself hidden by a bandstand and the clumps of trees growing thickly nearby. At such times it was not difficult for the children to make believe that he was indeed the Governor, and that these were his private grounds. There was something truly proprietorial about Mr Green as he stood there, oblivious of their presence, hostage to some troubling recollection. However, a gust of wind through the trees or a fight among the children and the melancholy would be set aside, to be resurrected and resumed the following Sunday.

His shadow stretched out before him on the path, the harshness of his dress muted in the softer light, he led them through an avenue of trees to the greenhouses where the more exotic exhibits were on display and there showed them insect-devouring plants, fruit one bite of which sufficed to kill a man, and a tree that 'bled'. Mr Green lingered over these things longer than the children cared for. The botanical gardens, so alien, so distinct, seemed hardly to connect with the street they had left three hours before. It was a swept, ordered profusion, a region of shadow on cut grass and strange fruit made stranger still by Mr Green's heady fascination for malignancies they did not understand and which appalled and frightened them. Some of the children cried, but Mr Green, ignoring, or perhaps ignorant of their distress, touched and smelled everything, delighting in the heat and spray of water from the pipes, his suit and helmet tinted green by the light filtering through the vines that crept up the sides of the glass and spread out over the roof. He would leave only when one of the caretakers looked in and told them it was time to go.

If these visits were not the undiluted pleasures they ought to have been, there were some advantages to be had in associating with Mr Green. He was a skilled carpenter and built stools and chairs and desks which he gave to the children. However, the most prized of all his accomplishments were the telephones he was able to make out of bits of wire and old tins. This sustained his popularity and at the same time it allowed him to continue his excursions to the zoo and botanical gardens.

Time having smoothed the rougher edges, the street learned to accept the Greens, bestowing on them the respect that springs from incomprehension. Crowds no longer gathered to watch Mrs Green paint, and although the men lounging on the corner still shouted 'Here comes the Governor', when Mr Green appeared dressed in his white suit, it was done less from malice than a desire to acknowledge his presence. Yet the Greens did come to have one thing in common with their neighbours: they shared their unchanging way of life. In that life, no one ever got richer or poorer; there were no dramatic successes or, for that matter, dramatic failures; no one was ever in serious trouble. Basically, they were cowards. Now and again Grant Street spawned a prodigy, a policeman for instance, but that was considered an aberration and did not happen often. Nevertheless, unheroic as it undoubtedly was, the street did have its heroes: the man in the Western who, flying in the face of the odds, conquers all, and his corollary, the loser, riding off, but with dignity, into the sunset.

The Greens succumbed to this pattern. The shoe-shop maintained a steady trickle of customers; Mrs Green continued to paint ships in distress and vases of flowers; the same silence swallowed now the husband, now the wife; and the tamarind tree, a prisoner of its own maturity, grew no taller. The changes Grant Street knew centred on the succession of carnivals, of births, and of deaths. Marriage, like the policeman, was an aberration that occurred infrequently. Ephemeral groups of children called Charlie and Yvonne and Sheila gathered round Mr Green and were introduced to the wonders of the zoo and botanical gardens and they cried as their predecessors had done. Mr Green, in his turn, saw them grow up, become mothers and putative fathers, fading away from him to the street corners and front steps of hovels.

Therefore when Mrs Green started work as a receptionist to a doctor it was considered almost an infringement of the established order, and when he was seen to come for her in the mornings and bring her back in the afternoons, it amounted to a disturbance of the peace. It soon became apparent that her suppressed passion had found an outlet. All the symptoms were there. When the doctor brought her back in the afternoon they talked long and earnestly in the car before he left, and Mrs Green, who, though distant had always been friendly, now abandoned her friendliness altogether. One change led to another. The painting sessions stopped and so did the visits to the library on Saturday mornings. From these occurrences was dated the commercialization that was to sweep Grant Street, as if there were some species of sympathetic magic at work connecting the two sets of events. And it certainly was the case that hard on the heels of Mrs Green's liaison the Pax Bar and grocery first made their appearance. Mr Green alone seemed unaware of what was happening. He worked in his shop as usual, smiled benignly at the children and took them out for walks. Unfortunately it was noted that he had recently begun to make more telephones than he had ever done. Mr Green's sadness ceased to be speculative. The street had its standards. There were limits to what anyone could do, and one of the unspoken rules in their relationship with Mr Green was that their standards did not apply to him: he had a role to fulfil. They felt not merely that his wife was 'wronging' him, but more peculiarly, that her manner of doing it was sordid. For them, morality was a matter of form, of 'style', and they did not approve of Mrs Green's style.

Grant Street's commercialization proceeded apace, and in the rush of cars and business and the sounds of the steelband, the Greens receded. The steelband was the

street's pride and had rapidly become the focus of its loyal-
ties. They practised every night and were good enough to
merit being recorded. The radio spread their fame and
eventually even the American tourists came to marvel at
the men who could produce such sweet and coherent sounds
from oil drums. Mr Green, his accomplishments thrown
into shadow by the influx of visitors, was deserted by his
youthful congregation. The telephones which he made in
increasing quantities lost their market and lay in untidy
heaps on top the trade magazine for 1950. He had to entice
the children into the shop and as before tried to talk to
those who did come about his life in Brazil and the daughter
he longed to see, but they were impatient and not interested
in these stories. Formerly, they had begged him for his
telephones and compliance had had to be dragged out of
him. Now to hold them in his shop he had to promise
instruments of greater sophistication. The next day he
would be sure to see his efforts abandoned in the gutter
outside his house or being kicked along the street. He stopped
making telephones and on Sundays he took his walks alone.
One or two people remembered to say, 'Here comes the
Governor', but it was done without any enthusiasm, and
Mr Green to avoid them went another way.

One morning some workmen arrived and they produced
the first noises to come from the Greens. A crowd gathered
on the pavement to watch. The house was being pulled
down. Mr Green was detached. He worked in his shop all
day amid the crashing of timber and galvanized iron sheets.
The doctor arrived to supervise the demolition, leaving
later with Mrs Green and two trunks, an action sufficiently
daring to mollify the neighbours. There was no silence for
Mr Green to return to that night. The house was already
roofless and instead he went to the Pax Bar.

Everyone there recognized him and looked up with
unconcealed surprise when he went in. He bought half a
bottle of rum and sat alone in a corner. He wore his white
suit and did not remove his cork hat. Towards morning

Mr Green shook himself and got up a little unsteadily from his chair. He fixed his hat more firmly on his head and felt his way across the room, holding on to the sides of tables and backs of chairs in his path. The few remaining drunks eyed him disconsolately. 'Good night, Governor.' Mr Green went out into the dark, empty street. A chain of red beacon lights punctured the blackness of the hills. Grant Street was unreal in the stillness. Gazing up at the street lamps and the shuttered houses he walked slowly back to the workshop. He fumbled for a long time before he found his keys. There was no light in the shop and he lit a candle. Half-made telephones littered the bench and table. He picked up one, held the receiver to his ear and laughed. The trade magazine caught his eye. He leafed through it, glancing at the advertisements. The Baltimore Shoe Corporation claimed to be able to 'fit all sizes and conform to all tastes'. Mr Green laughed again and put the magazine back on the table. He closed the door, snuffed the candle and went to sleep on the floor.

When he awoke the demolition men were already at work. The doctor was giving them instructions. Mr Green examined his suit in the semi-darkness. It had changed colour, and circular brown patches showed where rum had fallen on it the night before. He started brushing it, then, frowning, he gave up the attempt. He opened late and worked until lunch-time, when he closed the shop and went to the Pax Bar. It was the last time Edwin Green, 'shoemaker and shoe-repairer', ever opened for business.

It was a small house and in three days the demolition was complete. The street salvaged what it could from the piles of timber laid out on the pavement. There was no one to stop them except the doctor, and even he, after an argument in which he called them 'carrion crows', allowed them to take what they wished. The new house took shape slowly. Grant Street had never seen anything like it. It was large and rambling in the Californian fashion, surrounded

by a lawn and fenced in from the street. The outside walls
were painted a bright pink, and wooden louvres were used
instead of windows. There were wrought iron gates surmounted by wrought iron lanterns. But by far the most
impressive innovation was the chimney on the roof.

Mrs Green returned when it was finished. She behaved as
if she had come to the street for the first time. In the afternoons she watered the lawn while the doctor fussed with
the potted plants and orchids which hung from the eaves.
Mr Green was banished to his reservation. His shop had
not been touched and stood in ramshackle and bizarre
opposition to the modernity that seemed poised to devour it.

The street had long ago surrendered its illusions about
him. The evidence to the contrary was too overwhelming,
and anyway they did not need these illusions. Mr Green's
fall had been public and obvious, and any private sorrow
which he might still have had could not compensate for or
hide his humiliation. Now all they could see was the
physical shell whose disintegration they studied with a
passive morbidity. Grant Street had a clear conscience.
It had expressed its sympathy for Mr Green and its horror
of what his wife was doing. There were many other things
demanding their attention.

Mr Green lived in the shop. His revelries in the Pax Bar
ended late in the evening, and as he crept down the street
on his way home he sang noisily, pausing to swear when his
steps stuttered uncontrollably. Occasionally he stumbled
and fell on the roadway and then he would lie there for
some minutes without moving. Sometimes he urinated as
he lay there, taking fresh swigs from the bottle he always
carried with him. He delivered his final orations outside
the shop, laughing and cursing in turn as he kicked at the
door until it gave way. Then, suddenly, he would fall silent
and leaning against the fence, stare at the freshly watered
lawn and the curtains in the new house drawn tight and
secure. At noon the next day he emerged, his suit tattered
and frayed beyond recognition, the cork hat dented and

twisted at an odd angle on his head, to make the journey once again to the Pax Bar. Mr Green's metamorphosis had been quickly absorbed into the landscape. The world had come to Grant Street and it would take more than the ragings of a drunken man to disturb them.

Sunday afternoon was hot. The men on the corner had sought the shade of the bookshop and in the yards children played and the women sat on their front steps fanning themselves and gossiping. The steelband maundered sleepily to itself; the Pax Bar would not open until evening. Grant Street was in limbo.

Tamarinds were in season and several children were collecting the fruit that had fallen off the tree and littered the yard in front of the shoe shop. Mr Green watched them from the doorway. His eyes were red and he blinked painfully in the harsh light. He reached for the bottle of rum on his work table, uncorked it and drank some. With a faint smile and still holding the bottle he approached the children gathering the tamarinds. He picked up a handful and offered it to one of the smaller girls. She shook her head and backing away began to cry. The other children retreated, dropping the fruit they had collected. Mr Green laughed, and stepped out on to the street. He looked at the house. The louvres were opened and even in the gloom he could see that the walls were covered with pictures. One stood out. It was a painting of a ship with only its rigging visible, on the verge of being totally annihilated by a mountainous sea. He threw the tamarinds in the gutter and started up the street. His walk was studied and tentative. The urine stains on his trousers showed clearly. He took another sip from the bottle and shielding his eyes from the sun he gazed up at the sky. There were only a few clouds about, and they were small and white. He quickened his pace when he saw the coconut seller turn the corner with his donkey cart.

The donkey, a shaggy, morose, under-fed creature, had

been tethered in a patch of weeds. Mr Green stopped to examine it. He passed his hands over its shanks and patted it. The men in the shelter of the bookshop laughed. Mr Green turned to address them. 'Do you call this a donkey? Poor creature. I've seen them in the wild ...' The rest of what he said was lost in their laughter. The coconut seller advanced on him. 'Mister, you better leave my donkey alone, or you go know what.' He traced patterns in the air with his cutlass. 'Friend, I was only pointing out ...' The coconut seller spluttered into obscenity and Mr Green, shaking his head sadly, drank some more rum and walked away.

On the Queen's Park Savannah people were playing cricket and football and horses were cantering on the exercise track near the racecourse. Families out for their Sunday walk paraded amiably on the perimeter. Mr Green sat on a bench under a tree and stared at them, eyes half-closed. A clock struck four. He was tired and sleepy and beads of sweat watered his face and arms. An attack of nausea frittered itself away, but the tiredness, reinforcing itself, would not go. He opened his eyes. There was a breeze and the dust was rising in clouds, hiding the horses and people. The colours of the sky and grass melted and footballers and cricketers wandered through a golden, jellied haze. A voice unattached to a body spoke near him, then receded. Someone tapped him on the shoulder. A dog played round his heels and barked from many miles away. Beyond the Savannah the sea was a sheet of light. The sun fled behind a cloud and the sea was grey and rose up to devour him. He shuddered. For a moment the disoriented world re-grouped, but it needed all his energy and all his will to keep it that way. He let it dissolve and shatter. The rum was everywhere, flowing from chimneys and lanterns and tumescent seas, soaking his clothes. He kicked feebly and the bottle rolled into the dust. He got up. The ground shivered. He swam to the iron railings protecting the Savannah from the road. Another dog barked, a herald

of the loneliness descending on all sides. Someone said,
'... back in time for dinner,' and someone laughed.
Weariness called on him to surrender, but he was already
on the road, creeping between the cars, and not far
away was a refuge of shaded green. A flag danced in the
sky. The brown, lifeless hills wavered. A gust of wind blew
through the trees; blossoms floated in the air; trees and
trunks and labels whirled towards him. The tree-lined
avenue was cooler and he was startled by his reflec-
tion looming up to meet him out of the foliage. In a
moment he was inside. There was a sound of spray, and
water dripped on to his hat and trickled down his face.
The desolation deepened. Stalks and flowers stumbled in
the effort to make themselves seen. He noticed the green
light flowing through the glass, becoming one with his
nausea, and he tried to remember why the children had
cried. The tree that bled. He moved towards it, but darkness closed in, confounding his desire, bringing with it
the smell of fruit even stranger than those he had described,
of flower-laden jungles and muddy rivers, landscapes of
the mind more real than any he had roamed. Then,
mercifully, there was only the darkness.

When the caretaker found him he had been dead for
an hour.

Two days later Mr Green was buried in the Mucurapo
cemetery. His body, contrary to custom, had been kept
in the funeral home, returning to Grant Street for the
brief religious service which was held in the drawing room
of the new house. Some hitherto unsuspected relations of
Mr Green turned up and wept, but no one from the street
was allowed in. They gathered on the pavement and stared
through the louvres at the coffin.

The procession did not have far to travel and a sombre
crowd of neighbours walked behind the hearse to the
cemetery. Mrs Green drove in a car. The sky clouded and
it began to rain, delaying the burial. It was already dark

by the time it was completed and the few limp wreaths had been scattered on the grave.

Within a month the workshop was pulled down – it took one morning to do the job – and for days afterwards the children played with the unreclaimed shoes that had been thrown in the gutter. The tide of grass invaded the spot where the shop had been, and the fence was extended.

Grant Street prospered. The borough council gave it concrete pavements and running water, and the Central Government, a sewage system. Commercialization had stimulated its ambitions and several of the residents built new houses, none of course as grand as the Enriques' (Mrs Green had remarried), but all with pretensions to modernity. The grocery had become a supermarket, the café a restaurant; and the steelband went on tours to the Bahamas and United States. Romantic relationships were regularized, and there were even a few marriages. Children were still numerous, but the index had changed: they were more numerous than motor cars.

The street had undergone a series of changes that went beyond carnival and birth and death, and this had brought nostalgia. Grant Street had acquired a past whose sharpness had been softened by the passage of time and now glowed with a gentle light. Those who were no longer there or had died shared that softness and were transfigured by it. Mr Green had left no physical reminder of his presence to trouble them and as a result his legend revived. His style of death, a memorial to his dreams, was beyond reproach, and in the end it redeemed him. Put in another way, in terms of the Westerns Grant Street loved, he had ridden into the sunset.

Shiva Naipaul

The Political
Education of
Clarissa Forbes

Clarissa Forbes had a mind of her own, a peculiarity sufficiently strange for her family to have recognized and sanctified it. The source of this independence of spirit was a mystery to her family, her friends, and, in due course, her employers. But first to bear the burden was her family.

The Forbes were poor and relatively humble. There had been a time when they were poorer and straightforwardly humble, but a new government had been voted into favour with help from people like the Forbes and in an initial flush of gratitude decided, among other things, to build new roads. The Forbes benefited from this.

Mr Forbes was a semi-skilled manual labourer, chronically out of work and compelled as a result to do jobs like sweeping the streets and cleaning windows, which he considered to be beneath his dignity. However, with the advent of the new government, the situation improved.

The extensive road-building programme left Mr Forbes with little spare time, but that spare time he spent not in a hovel wracked by the coming and going of cars and lorries, but in a new house, another of the government's gifts to its supporters, laid out side by side with other houses minutely similar to itself and inhabited by people indistinguishable from the Forbes.

Mr Forbes was understanding. 'If we was not all the same, there is bound to be some unreasonable people who go be sure to get up and ask why Tom different from Dick and Dick different from Harry. This way, nobody have reason to complain and we all happy.'

Mr Forbes was only partly right. True, his wife was happy. She applauded these sentiments. 'If everybody was like you, Ethélbert, there wouldn't be no trouble in this world today.' Clarissa, however, was less easily swept off her feet.

'Huh. I just don't understand people like you two. Is as if you have no sense of pride, no dignity, wanting to live and be just like all these foolish people you see around you.' She was sprawled on the sofa reading a copy of a cheap English magazine given her by a school friend whose aunt had emigrated to England.

'But what you mean, Clary?' her father objected gently. 'Don't tell me you prefer that other place we used to live in.'

'I do in a way, if you must know. At least there we was different, not living exactly like everybody else.'

'I just don't understand you, Clary.' Mr Forbes scratched his thinning hair, always a sign of perplexity. His tone, nevertheless, was mild and questioning. The disharmony his daughter had injected into the idyll he had been paint-ing was not an entirely unfamiliar experience.

'Well take this, for instance.' Clarissa flourished the cheap English magazine. There was a picture on the cover of a woman in a bikini, sitting on a rock and gazing into the far distance. 'You should read this and get an idea of how other people does live abroad, the different kinds of thing they does do.' Clarissa sat up. 'You know, over there they does go to places like Spain and Portugal for they holidays. Have a look at that.' She thrust the magazine near her father's face and showed him another photograph, this one in colour. It was a picture of dozens of pale-skinned people gathered round the edges of a swimming pool. The sea, in the distance, was hidden by a jungle of um-brellas. 'Tell me, where we does go for we holidays?' I never even set foot in Tobago once in my life. We never hear of that kind of thing. But over there they does take it for granted.'

Mr Forbes studied the photograph carefully. 'It look very nice', he said. 'Let me see it, Ethélbert.' Mr Forbes gave his wife the magazine. 'Yes. Ethélbert right. It look very nice.'

Clarissa snatched the magazine from her mother. 'You don't have to tell me that. I know it nice.' She flicked through the pages of the magazine in search of further evidence. 'Ah yes. All you ever hear of Torremolinos?' Her parents shook their heads. 'I thought so. That's exactly the kind of ignorance I mean. And another thing. Here we only have horse racing, not so?' Her parents nodded. 'Well over there in England they have something else. Greyhounds. You ever hear of that?'

Mr Forbes scratched his head. 'Greyhound is a kind of dog, not so?'

'That's right, Pa. You smarter than I thought. Everybody does go to the dog races over there.'

'Dog races?' Mrs Forbes was incredulous. 'You mean they does race dogs against each other?'

'I remember now,' Mr Forbes said. 'They does call it greyhound racing.' Mr Forbes was pleased with himself, hoping this display of knowledge would further impress his daughter.

'That's right, Pa. I glad to see you know a few things.'

'And they have jockey riding these dog?' Mrs Forbes inquired.

Mr Forbes laughed loudly, slapping his thigh.

'No, Ma. They does have an electric hare out in front which the dogs does chase around a track.'

Mrs Forbes did not fully understand, but she was happy to let the matter drop. Mr Forbes, however, was determined to press home his advantage. 'Hear she. Jockey riding dog. Have to be a very small jockey or a very big dog.' He spluttered into fresh laughter.

Clarissa warmed to her theme. 'Someone like you, Ma,

if you was living in England, could go in the evening to one of them bingo halls.'

'You mean they have places where they does only play bingo?'

'Every night without fail,' Clarissa assured her.

Mr Forbes whistled. 'I could go to the dog races and Maisie could go to them bingo halls.'

'Exactly,' Clarissa replied.

'I think I would really like them bingo halls.' Mrs Forbes, closing her eyes, surrendered to the seductive pictures of her imagination.

After this the Forbes were more circumspect in singing the praises of their new home in front of their daughter. Each new issue of the cheap English magazine brought its fresh dose of invective and a further unsettling of the Forbes household. To avoid this, Mr and Mrs Forbes did as much as was within their power to placate Clarissa. They responded with the same look of simple-minded amazement to everything she said, the same expressions of astonished incredulity and the same anxiety lest their ignorance should annoy her. Unhappily, try as they might, they could never quite escape the taint, imposed on them by the limitations, the 'inferiority' as Clarissa never tired of describing it, of their situation.

Nevertheless, Mr Forbes's political consciousness continued to grow, doubtless stimulated in part by his daughter's incessant attacks. Despite Clarissa's scorn or, most probably, because of it, he developed in response to the pleadings of the politicians a sense of the injustices done to him in years, centuries, gone by. And this by the very people Clarissa would have him imitate. For the moment, however, he was reticent. Mr Forbes was still unsure of his ground.

This process the Prime Minister called 'political education', and to put his loyalty beyond all reasonable doubt and also as an expression of his gratitude for all the Government had done for him, Mr Forbes joined the Party. He adopted its tie, whose motif was a yellow sun (presumably rising) over a blue sea. For some time Mr Forbes kept this a secret from Clarissa and listened in silent submission to her ravings about Torremolinos, the greyhound races and the bingo halls. But as the months passed his confidence grew and he began wearing his tie on Sundays when he went to the local Anglican church with his wife. Clarissa did not accompany them. 'It too low class,' she told her parents. 'If I go to any church at all it got to be Catholic.'

Mr Forbes was an admirable pupil. 'Nowadays,' he said to his wife, 'it ain't have a soul who going to push we around like they used to before. Let them just try it and the P.M. go take care of them.' Then he explained the facts about slavery and colonialism as described by the Prime Minister. Mrs Forbes applauded and was unable to decide who she loved more, her husband or the Prime Minister. In time, Mr Forbes joined the ranks of the active Party workers and scoured the countryside showering leaflets on the peasants. His enthusiasm stimulated gossip about the Party nominating him to run for the local council. Unfortunately though to Clarissa's unbounded relief, he was not chosen. She was aware that people in the best circles rather despised the proletarian character of the present Government and her father's activities had consequently become a great drain on her pride. Clarissa reproached him.

'You mean after all I teach you, you still think that running for the local council is the greatest thing in the world?'

Mr Forbes was apologetic. 'I didn't have anything to do with it, Clary. It was other people who was talking, not me.'

'People like you will never learn,' Clarissa said despairingly.

Mr Forbes hid his disappointment well and vowed to his wife that he would continue to serve the Party faithfully. Mrs Forbes, however, was greatly distressed by the turn of events and her fervour for the Prime Minister abated perceptibly.

'You been working for these people so long, Ethélbert, breaking your back to please them. You would think they could at least give you a seat on the Council as a kind of reward.'

'These decisions have to go through a lot of channels we don't know about, Maisie, and I feel sure that if they didn't give me a seat it was for a very good reason.'

'But you would think the Prime Minister ...'

Mr Forbes waved his hands angrily. 'He don't have nothing to do with this. You think he ever even hear my name? He is a busy man. And another thing, if I was a councillor I couldn't take you with me to functions and things like that. Is not that I insulting you, but you don't have ...' Mr Forbes, scratching his head, searched for the right words.

'I know what you mean, Ethélbert. But you could have take Clary with you.' Mrs Forbes was not used to compliments and by the same token she was only able to recognize the crudest insults. Political Education had hardly made any impact on her.

'Me!' Clarissa cried, looking up with a start from her magazine, 'Me! What you take me for, Ma?'

'Your mother was only using you as an example, Clary.' Mr Forbes was embarrassed.

'I hope so! I really hope so! Anyway, what's the point in working yourself up over a stupid thing like that for? Who would want to be councillor in a stupid place like this? If you was in Port-of-Spain I could understand. But in a place like Paradise. It beats me!' She gave the rocker on which she was sitting a gentle push with her feet and creaking demurely back and forth continued reading her magazine.

Mr Forbes, catching his wife's eye, shook his head sadly. In a world where the cheap English magazine was not to be denied, the Forbes, husband and wife, had come to feel themselves and their activities insignificant and Lilliputian. They began to wish Clarissa would leave home.

The object of their concern was not particularly pre-possessing. Clarissa's face was moon-shaped and faintly scarred by chicken-pox. Her round, black eyes were heavy-lidded and hemmed in by the bulging flesh that pressed in upon them from her cheeks. She had a boxer's build, squat and thick-set, her diaphragm giving the impression of having been added to the rest of her as an afterthought. As a result, one thought of it as being misplaced, another person's property which Clarissa had appropriated and turned to her own uses. Yet it was the attentions allegedly paid to this unlovely exterior which ultimately were to lead to the gratification of her parents' unspoken wish.

Clarissa, despite her irredeemable unattractiveness, took great care with her appearance. She was extremely vain. This, however, had not always been the case. As a child, she had shown little inclination to improve upon her looks and indeed, up to about the age of sixteen she had tended to emphasize her ugliness by the clothes she wore and the way in which she carried herself. Clarissa had, in other words, made a fetish of her ugliness. Then she met the girl whose aunt had emigrated to England and who, unaware of the revolution it would stimulate, introduced her to the cheap English magazine. Overnight Clarissa's world was transformed.

The first symptom of this transformation was her obsession with personal hygiene. Her cleanliness became mythical. She bathed twice each day, once in the morning before she went to school, and again in the evening before she went to bed, when, to the never-ending wonderment of her parents, she followed the exhortations of the tooth-paste manufacturers and brushed her teeth as well.

Her clothes, which she now chose with the greatest care, were always neat and well-ironed and her hair, which formerly she kept plaited close to her scalp, she let down and attempted to comb straight with the assistance of the village hairdresser. Clarissa took copies of the English magazine to her and explained she would like it done just as in the particular photograph that had caught her fancy.

'That style not make for hair like ours, Clarissa.' The hairdresser herself had adopted an 'African' hairstyle. Her political education was well advanced.

'I don't see why. Why only they must have it for?'

'Because they have softer hair than we, Clarissa. That's why. Look, I'll draw a picture so that you could see the difference.' The hairdresser illustrated the difference with two rough diagrams. 'You see how theirs does fall without any trouble? Now you try doing that to ours and see what go happen.'

Clarissa twisted her face sourly and glanced quickly away from the sheet of paper. 'You only making that up,' she said. 'You just like my father. I don't see why you can't use a really hot comb. That bound to get it straight.'

'But it might burn you.'

'I don't care. Is my head that go be burning. Not yours.' Clarissa stared wistfully at the photograph in the magazine.

The hairdresser was resigned. She did as she was told and applied a very hot comb. Clarissa grimaced but did not complain. 'You see what I tell you,' she said, gritting her teeth, 'our hair not really all that different.' The hairdresser was silent. When it was all over, she brought a mirror and Clarissa examined the result. Her cheerfulness disintegrated instantly. 'You call yourself a hairdresser? Like you out to spite me or something?' She began to cry.

'You looking just like one of them Amerindians you does see in British Guiana,' the hairdresser giggled. And then, being a woman of some sensitivity, she realized her mistake and added, 'I was only joking, Clarissa. Don't mind me. It not looking all that bad.' She compared it with the picture in the magazine. The resemblance was tenuous. 'I could fix it up for you in no time at all.'

'You do it on purpose,' Clarissa sobbed. 'You was jealous of me. Everybody in this place jealous of me. You 'fraid that I was going to look too pretty, so you take the chance of spiting me.'

The hairdresser endeavoured to soothe her. 'Come, Clarissa. Don't cry. I'll fix it up for you so it wouldn't look too bad. I'll give it a few curls and it will look real nice. You wait and see.'

Thus Clarissa had no alternative but to submit to a more discreet hairstyle, more in keeping, as the hairdresser put it, 'with our stiff kind of hair'. In the end, all was forgiven. Paradise had no other hairdresser.

However, Clarissa's programme was not confined to improving her appearance. She stopped going to any and every film that happened to be on at the village cinema. Now she went only to light American melodramas and musicals; every other kind of film she considered beneath her. Westerns, especially, she condemned as 'unrefined'.

In addition, many of her friends fell under the withering contempt of Clarissa's new austerity. One of the few survivors was the girl whose aunt had emigrated to England. Without her, Clarissa's supply of the cheap English magazine would have been strangled at its source. Her reputation in the village grew. Young men took to roaming near the house in the hope of catching a glimpse of the renovated Clarissa and their girlfriends, when they saw her on the street, usually on her way to school or, if to the hairdresser's, with a copy of the magazine rolled under her arm, shrieked insults at her: the kind of insults which Mrs Forbes would have had no trouble in understanding.

Clarissa thrived. Her favourite place of repose was the little verandah at the front of the house where, in the afternoons after she had returned from school, she rocked gently in the sunlight, filing her nails and reading. The boys would arrive on bicycles and leaning against the gate try to hold her in conversation.

'Hey, Miss Forbes, give we a smile, eh!'

'You looking real sweet today. How about a little kiss?'

Clarissa would frown into her magazine, brushing

imaginary flies away from her face. Then, with a shiver of annoyance, when the chorus seemed on the verge of melting away, she would rise and say, 'I don't see why you hooligans can't leave decent people alone. I can't even read in peace in my own house now.' And she would flounce inside, slamming the front door.

Clarissa's academic pretensions were never very great, but she took a stubborn pride in her poor performances, refusing to believe that they indicated any more than her own preoccupation with matters of greater importance and the spiritless mediocrity of those around her.

One day she returned home from school earlier than usual, and throwing her books on the floor, collapsed on the sofa with apparent disgust. Mrs Forbes was concerned. 'Clary! You sick or something?'

'Sick! I wish I was.' She stared at the books scattered on the floor. 'It's not me who sick, Ma. Is the people who live in this town sick, if you ask me.' She searched in her pocket for her nail file.

'Somebody trying to take advantage of you?'

'He would have if I had given him half a chance. Vulgar beast!' She filed minutely at her nails.

'Who you talking 'bout?' Mrs Forbes knelt down and began collecting the books.

'One of them masters at school. He was trying to be fast with me this afternoon.'

'You mean ...' Mrs Forbes gazed in scandalized disbelief at her daughter.

'That's right, Ma. If I had give him half a chance he would have rape me right there and then.' Clarissa studied the neat edges of her nails. She did not appear to be particularly shocked or distressed. She relished using the word 'rape' and Mrs Forbes, consequently, was inclined to treat what had happened as merely an echo from that larger, melodramatic world which Clarissa inhabited. It paralysed her normal response.

'I going to leave that school,' Clarissa added. 'I can't stay there after today. Anyway, that place don't have anything for me.' She replaced the file in her pocket and hugged herself. 'God! I can't tell you how much I wish I was abroad some place. Torremolinos. That's where I should have been born.'

'But that kind of thing might still happen there, Clary,' Mrs Forbes ventured timidly.

Clarissa was appalled. 'People like you does never learn,' she said. 'How many times I have to tell you things different over there?'

Mrs Forbes acknowledged her mistake and said no more.

Mr Forbes's reaction when he heard the news (he had been to a Party meeting) was similar to his wife's, but nevertheless he felt it his duty to go and see the schoolmaster. Clarissa was not pleased.

'What's the point of doing that, Pa? I leaving the place after all and I didn't even give the man a chance to touch me. I suppose he was just overcome by desire. That does happen to men sometimes, you know. I sure even you does feel like that sometimes.'

Mr Forbes was enveloped in a thickening mental fog. 'Overcome by desire.' Attempting to gain a securer foothold, he pushed it away from his mind. 'All the same,' he continued tentatively, 'it not right to have a man teaching there who is liable at any time to grab you in the corridor and . . .'

'I didn't say anything about a corridor, Pa. Maybe he's frustrated.'

'Look here,' Mr Forbes replied with abrupt resolution, 'I going to have it out with that man whether he frus . . . whether he is like what you say he is or not.'

The schoolmaster was jovial about the affair. 'I don't know how Clarissa get an idea like that into she head, Mr Forbes. I treat she the same as I does treat all my pupils. And anyway, she tell me the other day that she was leaving school, so I thought I could ask she to go and see a film with me. Mind you, if she was still going to be my pupil I would never have dream of doing a thing like that. It wouldn't have been ethical, if you see what I mean.' He gestured attractively with his cream-coloured palms. 'Not ethical at all, Mr Forbes. But I don't see where she get this idea about my wanting to rape she from. Is not a nice thing to say about a man, you know, Mr Forbes. Is not a nice thing to say at all. That kind of gossip could ruin people, especially a man in my position.' He rubbed his palms together, wagging his head mournfully from side to side.

Mr Forbes was convinced by the sincerity of this defence and he returned home to Clarissa worried and confused.

'He say he only ask you to go to a film, Clary. And besides you had make up your mind to leave school. You didn't tell we anything about that.'

Clarissa shrugged her shoulders. 'That's not the point,' she replied, but did not bother to elaborate.

'Anyway,' Mr Forbes persisted, 'it would have been unethical for him to try and do a thing like that.'

'I don't like all them big words,' Clarissa said, 'and anyway, I don't like talking about such things. It's better to leave that sort of thing to the other girls. Let them keep their "men".' She twisted her mouth in distaste. 'If I ever go with anybody it will have to be for love and love alone. I'll only become pregnant in wedlock.'

Clarissa's alternating use of the vernacular and that other vocabulary which stifled the judgement baffled Mr Forbes. Torn between the crudity of the former and the elegance of the latter, he listened uneasily to his daughter. Again he strove for the concrete.

'But did he really try to ... to ...' Mr Forbes scratched his head and avoided looking at his daughter.

'Really, Pa! Next you go be accusing me of lying.'

'Well I just wanted to ...'

'If you must doubt me. Yes. He did want to have sexual intercourse with me. But I'm a virgin and will remain one until the day I get married.'

Mr Forbes's perplexity deepened. Sexual intercourse. Virgin. The gap between him and his daughter widened. It was not Clarissa's knowledge of the world that worried him: it was the way she communicated this knowledge. Somehow she managed to make the world seem a much more threatening and mysterious place than he had ever imagined it to be. He dropped the matter and awaited with mounting impatience Clarissa's decision to leave home and begin that inevitable pilgrimage to the land of her dreams.

For some weeks, however, Clarissa did nothing. She remained at home, clean and fragrant, rocking with determined obstinacy on the verandah, occasionally taking time off to rail at the smallness and pettiness of Paradise.

'Look at this place,' she exclaimed, 'a main road with a lot of houses on either side. What do they expect people to live here and do, eh?'

'Me and your father live here all we life. We never complain about it,' her mother answered.

'That's because you and he have no ambition.'

For the first time, Mr Forbes lost his temper.

'It's because we know we place. For people like we it all right, but for people like you ... well, you could only make trouble for yourself and everybody else. You is the sort of person who have to wait for people to spit in your face before you come to your senses.' Mr Forbes watched his daughter narrowly. 'Why don't you go to Port-of-Spain then and live with your aunt?'

'With Auntie Selma! You must be crazy or something, Pa. She does live in John-John with all kinds of louts and riff-raff. What you take me for, Pa?'

'You might find a nice job there and get married,' Mr Forbes went on. His tone was simultaneously conciliatory and goading.

'I could see you out to insult me, Pa. If all you want to do is get rid of me why don't you say so right out instead of beating round the bush?'

'Who say we want to get rid of you?' Mr Forbes replied soothingly.

'Get married!' Clarissa snorted. 'What do you take me for, eh? You think I like all these girls you see running round Paradise?'

'Nobody say that. We know you different.'

'I'll make up my mind in my own good time, you hear. Nobody going to push me around.'

Nevertheless, Clarissa announced her decision the following week.

'I think I'll go and find work in Port-of-Spain after all. I sure to meet a different class of people there.'

'That's a good idea, Clary,' Mr Forbes said.

'You don't have to tell me that, Pa. I know.' Clarissa was filing her nails. 'I'll go and be a nurse to some rich people children. They does do that kind of thing down there, treating you like one of the family.'

'You need qualifications to be a nurse.' Mr Forbes fingered his Party tie. Political education had gradually enlarged his idea of the complexity of things (due in large part to his failure to gain a seat on the local council) and he derived some comfort from being able to hint at the snags in any undertaking.

'I will learn, Pa. I not stupid you know.'

In Port-of-Spain, Clarissa discovered that while the wealthy did indeed want 'nurses', they were, none of them, prepared to treat her as one of the family. She would be subject to all sorts of regulations and restrictions which, needless to say, she found offensive. The charms of the Opposition faded and she detected in her heart small, but undeniably sympathetic sentiments towards the Government. Clarissa, however, was not yet prepared to surrender to these baser instincts. She would compromise.

Day after day she ran her finger down the classified column of the newspaper. Too many of them asked for 'servant'. That was taking compromise too far, since for

Clarissa it was metaphor alone that made the present world habitable. She persevered until at last she noticed that the Gokhools wanted a 'maid'. Clarissa arranged to be interviewed.

The Gokhools lived in a large, rambling house in Woodlands. It was surrounded by a well-watered lawn and two cars were parked in the garage. She hesitated on the pavement, studying the other houses on the street, nearly all as prosperous as the Gokhools'. Unconsciously she had allowed an expression of mild astonishment to form on her face, then, suspecting this, her eyes narrowed into a harder stare.

She rattled the gate. A small white dog came bounding out of the house, barking furiously, a frail woman in pursuit. 'Stop that, Nelson. Get back to your kennel.'

Nelson, ignoring her, barked frenziedly at Clarissa.

The woman looked at Clarissa. 'You are the girl who come for the servant job we advertise?'

Clarissa, shrinking into her obstinacy, nodded briefly.

'Come inside, then. Nelson bark is a lot worse than his bite. Pedigree dogs tend to be rather highly-strung, you know.' The woman tittered, and Clarissa opened the gate, her hostility focused on the yapping dog. Nelson subsided instantly, cowering behind the woman who had bent down to stroke him.

'So you are the girl, eh?' She examined Clarissa's clothes with the barest slinking displeasure. 'You ever do servant-work before?'

Clarissa shook her head, gazing, her eyes dull and lifeless, at the woman crouched at her feet.

'I'm Mrs Gokhool.' The woman stood up, smoothing her skirt. 'Come this way into the kitchen where we can talk.' Mrs Gokhool, adopting a more business-like manner, led the way briskly, leaving a faint trail of perfume in her wake. Clarissa shambled negligently behind her. They entered the kitchen, a spacious tiled room, obviously newly built. All the equipment was electric and extremely modern. Clarissa had to struggle to control the look of astonishment that was about to descend on her again. The expression she assumed implied that nothing could surprise her. Mrs Gokhool threw herself into a chair.

'We had to send the last girl away because she got pregnant.' Mrs Gokhool twirled a strand of her hair around her fingers. 'She was having a baby, that is,' she explained, smiling more genially at Clarissa. 'My husband didn't want to have yet another mouth to feed and anyway she started having all kinds of riff-raff hanging round the house. It's amazing how quickly that kind of thing can happen. Overnight.' Mrs Gokhool wrinkled her brows and smiled up at Clarissa. 'But I don't expect you are the sort of girl to go and do a thing like that.' As she had done earlier, she glanced at Clarissa's clothes with the same hint of muted displeasure. 'Still,' she waved her hands, running her eyes over the shining kitchen equipment, 'all that's over and done with now, thank God.' She sighed. 'Well, I suppose what you really want to know is what your duties would be if we decide to give you the job.'

Clarissa stood withdrawn and unmoved before Mrs Gokhool.

'You wouldn't have to do any cooking. I have someone else for that.' Mrs Gokhool paused, waiting for a reaction, but none forthcoming, she went on. 'But you would have to help with the washing up. Adeleine suffers from rheumatism and it's not good for her to be in water too much.'

Clarissa's gaze travelled over the varnished wooden ceiling, returning to rest for an instant on the tip of Mrs Gokhool's nose, before settling on the floor. She gave the impression of not having heard a word.

'Your main job, though, would be the cleaning of the house, the making of the beds in the morning and looking after the children generally. Saturday afternoons will be yours and you can do anything you want then, within reason of course. There's a cinema just across the road.'

Clarissa had drawn herself tightly together as if striving

to efface the image of the woman speaking to her. Nelson came running into the kitchen and crawled under the table. Mrs Gokhool picked him up and put him on her lap. She stroked his long, furry ears. 'Naughty boy. I thought I told you to go to your kennel.' She turned to Clarissa. 'You just leave school?'

'Uh huh.'

'Your parents still alive? This last girl we send away was from the Belmont Orphanage.'

'Uh huh.'

'What does your father do?'

'He's a councillor.' Clarissa hardly parted her lips as she spoke and the sounds emerged as if wrapped in cotton-wool.

Mrs Gokhool, herself a supporter of the Opposition, was condescending.

'A councillor! That's nice. So you come from an important family?' She grinned at Clarissa.

Clarissa twisted her face sourly. She did not answer the question. Instead she asked whether she would have a room of her own if she, and Clarissa laid special emphasis on this, if she 'decided to take the job'.

Mrs Gokhool looked at her queerly. 'Yes, yes. I was forgetting. Come and I'll show you.' She got up hurriedly, Nelson sliding from her lap, and went out through another door into the backyard and pointed at a small, low shed with a corrugated iron roof kept in position by strategically placed stones. Next to it was Nelson's kennel with 'Home Sweet Home' painted in neat red letters on the front. Clarissa stared at it, trying to disguise her interest. She had never seen a kennel before, not even in the cheap English magazine.

'It's not as bad as it looks,' Mrs Gokhool grinned cheerfully at Clarissa. She was referring to the shed, not the kennel. 'It's much better inside than out and it has everything you will need. The other girl was very happy until she began getting ideas above her station.'

They went inside, having to stoop slightly so as not to

brush against the roof. The shed was furnished with a bed and a battered wardrobe. Along one wall there was a sagging bookshelf, filled with old text-books. The floor was of bare concrete and there was no electric light. 'You will have to use candles, but I don't suppose you do much reading anyway, so that doesn't matter.'

'I read a lot,' Clarissa said.

'Do you? Oh, I forgot to ask. What's your name?'

'Clarissa.'

'What do you read, Clarissa?'

'All kinds of things.'

Mrs Gokhool giggled. 'Well, you won't have much time for that here, Clarissa. But what little reading you like doing you can do in the daytime. It's a nice little room, don't you think? The electric light is the only drawback.'

What Clarissa thought was written plainly on her face. She did not attempt to hide her disappointment. She puffed out her cheeks and with that look of sourness that had become habitual to her, stared morosely round her future surroundings, refusing to be drawn by Mrs Gokhool's forced enthusiasm.

Mrs Gokhool giggled uncomfortably. 'It used to be a chicken-run at one time.' They went out into the yard.

'When do you think you can start work? If you want the job, that is. I have lots of other girls like you breathing down my neck.'

'Tomorrow. I can start tomorrow.' Nelson sniffed at her heels.

Mrs Gokhool promised to have the room cleaned. 'I'm sure you will like the rest of the family. My husband is the easiest man in the world to get on with, once you do your work properly.' Mrs Gokhool escorted her to the gate. 'Till tomorrow then, Clarissa.'

'So you going to be a nurse after all,' Mr Forbes mused. 'Well, I must say that really surprise me.'

'I keep telling you I not stupid like you think.' Clarissa

was arranging her clothes with great care in a suitcase.
'People know they can't push me around.'

'They giving you a uniform to wear?' her mother asked.

'Nothing like that, Ma. The woman say they going to
regard me as one of the family. Mind you, I don't think I
going to stay with them all that long. What I really want to
do is a commercial course.'

'But you haven't even start the job as yet and you already
talking about leaving. You is a funny girl, Clary.' Mr Forbes
scratched his head.

'A long time ago I set my heart on a commercial course. I
don't want to be a . . . a nurse for the rest of my life.'

'What you want to do a commercial course for?'

'What do you mean, Pa? I going to be a top class secretary one of these days. I don't mean any ordinary secretary
like you does see running about all over the place. I mean
really top class. I intend to work in a bank or something
like that.'

'You ever see a black person working in a bank?'

'You wait and see,' Clarissa said. 'Mrs Gokhool say she
going to use she influence to find me a really first-class job
some place. They is important people, you know.'

'They sound really nice. You is a lucky girl, Clary.' Mrs
Forbes looked at her daughter admiringly.

'People know they can't push me around,' Clarissa
insisted.

Clarissa and the Gokhools were destined not to like each
other. At almost every point her duty came into conflict
with her dignity. They quarrelled on the first day when Mrs
Gokhool insisted that she wear a special blue and white
uniform when taking the children for walks. Clarissa
refused.

'I don't want everybody taking me for a common servant,
Mrs Gokhool.'

'But what do you think you are, Clarissa? You mustn't
forget that I am employing you. Just because your father is

on some borough council or other and you want to take a commercial course – I don't know who put that idea into your little head – that doesn't make any difference you know.'

'I not a common servant Mrs Gokhool and you wait and see, I going to take a commercial course, no matter what you say.'

'Why you working for me then? I didn't ask you to take the job. If you feel like that you shouldn't have come here in the first place.'

'I doing a job for money, Mrs Gokhool. But I not nobody's servant. I won't let anybody kick me around.'

'You must be mad.'

In the end it was Mrs Gokhool who capitulated and Clarissa took the children for walks dressed as she pleased. She avoided those places where the other 'maids' on the street congregated with their charges; but, in the succeeding weeks inevitably having to meet and talk with them, let fall that she was a friend of the family and doing them a favour. Thus having established her position relative to them, they no longer sought to chat and gossip with her about their employers. However, the full flight of Clarissa's fancy was reserved for the rheumatic Adeleine with whom she was in daily contact.

'I'm really a kind of au pair girl,' Clarissa told her.

'A what?' Adeleine had not heard of such things before.

'An au pair girl. They have them in places like England and that.'

'Oh. But I never hear of them in Trinidad before, Clarissa.' Adeleine was as guileless as Mrs Forbes, slow to suspect or take offence and willing to believe anything she was told.

'Is not a common thing as yet. But it just starting to happen here. I'm not really a servant at all, you see.'

'I understand now. But ...' a doubt formulated itself hesitantly in Adeleine's mind, an unusual thing with her, 'but I don't see you eating with them and things like that. You does eat in the kitchen just like me and that other girl who used to be here. How is that?'

'That's because,' Clarissa replied readily, 'I like keeping myself to myself. I don't like mixing with all different kinds of people. I is a fussy person. I like to pick and choose.'

Adeleine nodded slowly. At last she understood. From then on she kept a suitable distance between Clarissa and herself.

These rumours drifted back to Mrs Gokhool. She liked them even less than Clarissa's refusal to wear a uniform. Nevertheless, she bided her time and said nothing. These stories were an unfailing source of amusement to her friends and they urged her to keep her on for a while longer. 'You can't get rid of such a gem,' they said.

But the causes for mutual complaint grew apace. Mrs Gokhool also read magazines, though of a different kind, and, like Clarissa, they were the source of many of her ideas on elegant living.

'I want you to call Jerry Master Jerry from now on,' she informed Clarissa one day. 'I don't think you should be so familiar with him.'

Clarissa laughed, unfeignedly astonished and amused by this latest directive. 'But I so much older than him,' she protested.

'That's not the point. At this rate you will be calling me Mavis soon.'

'You older than me. But Jerry?' She burst out laughing again.

'Master Jerry.'

'But Jerry . . .'

'Master Jerry.'

'. . . he not even ten years old and I is seventeen.' Clarissa puffed out her cheeks, shaking her head, and Mrs Gokhool knew she had lost again. She did not retail this 'story' to her friends. It was embarrassing and she was not even sure whether they would approve. They might laugh at her, not at Clarissa. Therefore this refusal rankled more than the rest.

Reluctant as she was to fall back on her father's political teachings, nevertheless Clarissa's injured pride fled there to nurture its grievances. She had divided her world into two quite separate spheres: a present full of injustice, a future laden with promise. The one fed the other. The nature of this future was unclear, except for her conviction that, in it, all wounds would be healed. In the meantime, hoping to further extend her horizons and prepare herself for that great day, she read, furtively, all Mrs Gokhool's American magazines and experimented with her expensive perfumes. Mrs Gokhool caught her. 'So, like you want to take my place as mistress of this house, Clarissa?'

'I was only trying the perfume out, Mrs Gokhool.'

'What make you think this kind of perfume is for you, child? That is proper French perfume you know. I just don't know who is putting all these grand ideas in your head.' She took the bottle away from Clarissa. 'This sort of thing wasn't meant for people like you.'

'I don't see why.' Clarissa puffed out her cheeks.

Mrs Gokhool stared at Clarissa for some moments without speaking. Her status had never been seriously called into question before. 'Get this into your head, girl. You are not like me. We are not the same kind of people.' She paused, scrutinizing Clarissa's face, before turning away discomfited by what she saw there. She lowered her voice. 'Look, here, Clarissa. I don't want you to feel I'm doing you down, but what I'm telling you is going to be for your own good. My husband is, as you must know, an important man. We belong to . . .' Mrs Gokhool groped for words, her eyes wandering painfully over the room.

'I know,' Clarissa replied. 'You believe that you is really high-class people and I is some kind of dirt which you can sweep anywhere you want. That was what you wanted to say, not so?'

'That is not what I want to say, Clarissa.' Mrs Gokhool's

composure was cracking fast. 'I've been very reasonable with you before now. Believe me when I say that none of the people I know would stand from a servant . . .'

'I is not a servant, Mrs Gokhool. I doing a job for money.'

'. . . none of them would stand from a servant what I have stood from you. You would've been out on your ears after two minutes.'

'I is not a servant,' Clarissa intoned, but she seemed to be trying to convince herself rather than Mrs Gokhool.

'. . . there was that business about Jerry for instance, then your telling everybody that you were a friend of the family. A friend of the family! And not wanting to wear a uniform . . .'

'I is not a servant . . .'

'. . . and what was that phrase you used? An au pair girl? For a servant you have a lot of false pride. Not wanting to call my son Master, well I never . . .'

Clarissa roused herself. 'I wouldn't call that boy Master if you was to pay me a million dollars. Not even for a million dollars, you hear.'

'Look here, girl!' Mrs Gokhool shouted suddenly. 'Watch how you talking to me. I'm not your equal, get that straight. My husband is a rich, important man. He has more money in his pocket alone than you will ever see in your entire life and I'm employing you and that means you are my servant. My servant. Get that straight in your head.'

'Having money don't make you God you know. And he only get that money by robbing poor people. But the Government going to fix all of you soon.'

'Who going to do that? Your councillor father? Is he going to come and dispossess us?'

'I warning you not to insult my father, Mrs Gokhool . . .'

Mrs Gokhool took a step nearer Clarissa. She spoke slowly, measuring each word. 'You are a servant, Clarissa, not a friend of the family as you keep lying to everybody on the street. A servant! A servant! A servant!'

'I'm not yours or anybody's servant, Mrs Gokhool. My father is a respectable man. He didn't want me to take this job in the first place and if he ever get to hear of the way you treating me ...' Clarissa lowered at her. Mrs Gokhool laughed shrilly.

'He's going to come and beat me up. Don't tell me.'

'That's the sort of thing only you would do.'

'Oh! So you are more respectable than us now. Good. I'm grateful to you for telling me. You have any work for me to do? Maybe I could wash your feet for you and spread a red carpet everywhere you walk.'

'I didn't come here for you to insult me, Mrs Gokhool.'

'Sorry, Miss Clarissa. Sorry.' Mrs Gokhool bowed her head low, bringing her palms together in mock obeisance. 'Well, I don't suppose we can continue to be honoured with your presence.'

'Don't think you can tell me to go, Mrs Gokhool. I make up my mind to leave here a long time ago.'

'Don't let us keep you, Miss Clarissa.'

'Stupid, stupid people,' Clarissa muttered and stumped heavily out of the room.

'Clarissa!' Mrs Forbes, astonished, watched her daughter come stumbling up the path. 'What happen?'

'I give up the job.' Her tone was matter of fact. She threw her suitcase on to the steps.

'But why? I thought they was such nice people wanting you to be like one of the family and that.'

'Nice people!' Clarissa spat, and pressing her lips tightly together, kicked the suitcase. 'They wanted me to be too much like one of the family, if you ask me. The woman husband try to rape me.'

'You mean to say ...'

'Exactly, Ma. You hit the nail on the head. He wanted to sleep with me.'

Mrs Forbes gazed more with puzzlement than with alarm at her daughter. 'Sleep with me.' The phrase echoed in her ears. She had never heard it put like that before. Her judgement clouded.

'Imagine that,' she murmured, unable to suppress the note of admiration creeping into her voice. 'Imagine that. A big, respectable man like that wanting to ... to sleep with you.'

Mr Forbes when told was tempted to intervene. Clarissa dissuaded him. 'It's not that important, Pa. After all, for a man, especially a frustrated man, to want to sleep with a woman is only natural.' And he too, falling victim to the magic phrase, decided the matter was outside his competence.

During the time she had been at the Gokhools', Clarissa had saved sufficient money to enable her to enrol for the commercial course she had long set her heart on. She relented on the matter of accommodation and in the end agreed to live rent-free with her Auntie Selma in Port-of-Spain.

'When I finish this course,' Clarissa declared, 'I could get a job anywhere in the world. And not any old job either. You mark my words.'

Clarissa bought all the necessary books and a fountain pen. The books she covered carefully with waterproof paper and her name she wrote on specially chosen pink and white labels. It looked extremely pretty. Each day Clarissa wore a different coloured cotton blouse and a neatly pressed skirt. She was the best dressed girl at the college, and for a month all went well. The reports she sent home were enthusiastic. She even dropped hints about being 'dated' by the man who ran the college. Her parents, poring over the cryptic language, marvelled at their daughter's success.

Unhappily Clarissa was dogged by the same kind of mediocrity that had crippled her performance at school, and, to make matters worse, thrifty though she had been at the Gokhools', she had been buying too many clothes and cosmetics and thus was unable to finance more than her first month's attendance. She was summoned by the head of the college.

'Now, Miss Forbes,' he said, 'you owe us fees for four weeks. We are not running a charity here, you know.'

'I expecting some money soon, Mr Roberts, in another month or so. I'll pay you then.'

Mr Roberts shook his head mournfully. 'A bird in the hand is worth two in the bush, Miss Forbes, and your birds are too much in the bush for my liking.' The phrase pleased him. He smiled dreamily, playing with his thin beard. 'I will tell you something, Miss Forbes. I was a very trusting man when I first began running this business and everybody was taking advantage of me right, left and centre. Hundreds of dollars are still owing to me all over the place. I'm sorry, but I must have it now.'

Clarissa fixed her eyes on the floor. 'I not the sort of person to run away without paying, Mr Roberts. Give me a chance. I'll be getting money soon.'

'I have heard that story too many times, Miss Forbes. Anyway, your work here doesn't justify my giving you a chance.'

Clarissa closed her eyes, her lips pinched together. She seemed to be trying to ward off some unpleasant image or memory.

'You mustn't think me hard-hearted, Miss Forbes, but I must draw the line somewhere.' He spoke as if from a prepared speech.

'I'll do anything you want me to do, Mr Roberts. Just give me one more chance.' Clarissa's eyes strayed over his face.

'What are you suggesting, Miss Forbes?'

Clarissa did not answer. Her eyes, leaving him, swept across the walls and ceiling.

'You're a nice girl, Miss Forbes, and you take a lot of care of yourself. I can see that. But don't go and spoil it . . .'

'I'll do anything you ask, Mr Roberts. Anything.' Clarissa no longer struggled to hold back her tears.

'No, Miss Forbes. That won't do. It's a bad policy to get ... how shall I put it? ... to get involved with one's students in this kind of business. I speak from bitter experience.' Mr Roberts, unruffled by her tears, stared steadily at Clarissa, displaying the professional concern of the undertaker.

'You is a stupid, stupid man. I could tell you how much people try to make it with me, getting down on they knees and begging me. Is not everybody I does offer myself to and don't think I haven't seen how you been watching me out of the corner of your eye these past few weeks.'

'I'm surprised to hear you talk like that, Miss Forbes. Truly surprised.' And he could not resist adding, 'If I was watching you it was only because you hadn't paid your fees.'

'You're a stupid, stupid man. Don't believe you will ever have another chance with me. I warning you. Your face not all that pretty.'

'I never said it was, Miss Forbes.' He got up. 'I think you better take your things and go. You can pay me when you get the money you were talking about.'

'You is a real nigger!' Clarissa screamed. 'Is people like you who is the cause of our people downfall, making everybody treat we like servant. They should throw you in jail. In jail, you hear!'

'Yes, Miss Forbes, I hear. But you better go now before you say anything you will really regret.' Mr Roberts pushed her gently towards the door.

'In jail, in jail,' Clarissa whimpered.

'Here, Miss Forbes. You are forgetting all your nice books.'

'You could eat the damn books, for all I care.' Clarissa brushed her tears away in quick, violent movements. Then, pushing him aside, she ran abruptly out of the room, slamming the door hard behind her.

Once more Mrs Forbes was confronted by the sight of her daughter struggling up the path with her suitcase.

'You finish the course already?' she asked.

'I give it up.'

'You give it up? But think of all that money you waste, Clary.'

'Is not my fault. Is the blasted man who own the school to blame.'

'You mean...'

'Yes. That's right. He try to rape me like the rest of them.'

Mrs Forbes nodded. This time Mr Forbes did not even suggest intervention.

Clarissa sought and found comfort in the pages of the cheap English magazine. However, she was altogether quieter and more withdrawn. Her parents, especially Mr Forbes, were distressed by the change in their daughter.

Mr Forbes was not an entirely stupid man. It struck him as distinctly odd that three quite different men at one time or another should have tried to rape his daughter. He studied her. She was not beautiful. He mentioned this to his wife and she agreed. 'I never think of it like that before,' she said. Mr Forbes brooded over Clarissa's history and, as he brooded, his distress gave way to ill-temper. His political education was by now very far advanced.

'Clary,' he said one day when she had been more than usually reticent, 'what would you say about my paying your passage to England?'

Clarissa brightened. 'You really mean that, Pa?'

'Yes.'

'That's the place I feel where I really belong. Living in a flat and that sort of thing.' Mr Forbes scowled. 'Mind you,' she went on, 'what with all that rain and fog and thing is not an easy life. But I really feel that's the kind of life I was made for. Still, it's expensive getting there.' She glanced doubtfully at her father.

'Not if you take one of them immigrant ships and travel third class.'

'Immigrant ships! Third class!' Clarissa flung the copy

of the magazine she was reading on to the floor. 'What do you take me for, Pa?'

'Shut up, child. You'll do as I say or not at all. I'm damn tired of all your stupid prancing around the place. Is high time you learn some respect for me.'

'Ethélbert!' Mrs Forbes groaned, alarmed at the prospect of their daughter's scorn falling on their heads. She worried needlessly. Clarissa did not rise to the bait. Her reply was defensive, self-pitying.

'You just like everybody else, Pa. Trying to take advantage of me.'

'Nobody taking advantage of you. Is your . . . is your . . .' He flung his arms about excitedly.

'Ethélbert,' Mrs Forbes groaned, 'don't excite yourself so.'

'Keep quiet, Maisie, and mind your own business.' He turned again to face Clarissa. 'Is your damn colonialist mentality that taking advantage of you. Yes, that's what it is. Your colonialist mentality.' It was a phrase the Prime Minister had employed recently against a renegade Minister who had embezzled large sums of money and fled to Switzerland. Mr Forbes waved a threatening finger in front of Clarissa's face.

'You always blaming your failure on people wanting to rape you. Well, let me tell you something. You got to have sex appeal for people to want to rape you and you have about as much of that as I have. But you go to England and we go hear how much of that kind of nonsense you go still be talking when you come back.' The magazine caught his eye. He picked it up from the floor and flipped rapidly through the pages. 'Is this what you consider so great? Is this where you does get all your stupid ideas from? You should be shamed of yourself. Let me see.' He read aloud from the magazine. 'They met on holiday in the Riviera, he, unmarried and bronzed as a Greek god, a happy-go-lucky man of the world, she, good-looking and with a husband suffering from leukaemia . . .'

'Give me back my magazine, Pa. What I read is my own business.' Clarissa lunged at him.

'Tell me first what all this Riviera business got to do with a little nigger girl like you, eh?'

'Give me back my magazine please. Please.' Clarissa wrung her hands. Mr Forbes let the magazine slip through his fingers and fall on to the floor. Clarissa picked it up and hugged it close to her bosom.

A few weeks later Clarissa took passage to England on an immigrant ship, third class.

London was not all Clarissa expected it to be. True, there were fogs and days when it drizzled without cessation. But the fogs were not as thick or as yellow as she had been led to imagine and there were many days when it did not rain. Neither did Clarissa share a flat with a friend. She lived in a bed-sitter in a dilapidated immigrant section of the city. Her landlord, a West Indian, charged her six pounds a week for it. It had peeling wallpaper, a leaking ceiling and a stove that filled the room with smoke. She had no friends. The cheap English magazine, and others like it, existed in abundance, but she had lost her taste for it. Where were the Greek gods? The leukaemia-stricken husbands? The world pictured there hardly corresponded with what she saw around her every day, and on the rare occasion when the veil did lift, Clarissa took fright and ran away.

She was two months finding a job, as a ticket collector on the Underground. Week after week she stood outside her cubicle, her hands stretched forth to trap the stream of tickets thrust at her. At nights she crept slowly back home, cooked supper and went to bed to the accompaniment of the trains that rattled past beneath her windows. Her landlord was sympathetic.

'I know how lonely it does get when you away from home so long and all by yourself. But you does get accustom in the end, like me.'

'I leave a good home to come to this,' Clarissa replied.

'My father is a councillor. He would dead if he was to see me living like this.'

'I been here ten years. Take me a long time to save up to buy this place.' He surveyed the decaying room with pride. 'Ten years,' he repeated. 'Is warming to meet a really nice local girl like you after such a long time. From the moment I set eyes on you I know you had class. Real class. What you say your father is?'

'A councillor.'

'A councillor. Yes. You is a girl with real class.' He put his hand on her shoulder. Clarissa did not protest. 'I tired of these English girl.' He felt her hair. Still Clarissa did not protest. The landlord grew bolder. He swayed slightly as he bent low over her.

'You want to sleep with me?' Clarissa asked suddenly.

The landlord, taken aback, laughed. 'Real class,' he said.

'You want to sleep with me?'

'What a funny girl you is.'

'You want . . .'

'Yes, yes.'

And so Clarissa Forbes lost her virginity. But it was not for love and certainly it was out of wedlock.

Clarissa worked hard and this time she did not spend her money on clothes and expensive perfumes.

'But what you killing yourself so for?' the landlord asked.

'I going back home. I saving up for a tourist-class passage.'

'But, Clarissa . . .'

'No, Frankie. You was enough.'

A few weeks later she was back home.

'You see them dogs race?' her mother asked.

'No, Ma.'

'No bingo halls either?'

'No, Ma.'

'And I don't suppose you ever get to that place you was telling we about. Torr . . . something or the other.'

'No, Ma. I didn't manage to get to Torremolinos.'

'And nobody try to . . .'

'No, Ma. Nobody try to rape me.'

'But like you didn't do anything at all while you was there?'

'It was too cold out there, Ma,' Clarissa replied. 'It was much too cold.'

Mr Forbes's political fortunes had improved during Clarissa's absence. Recognition of his unswerving devotion to the Party came eventually and he was, after all, elected to the county council. Clarissa was proud of her father, and Mrs Forbes, whose ignorance was still an embarrassment to her husband, gratefully gave way to Clarissa who accompanied him on all important official occasions. And thus she too was brought to the attention of the branch Party. Her international experience stood her in good stead.

'We need more people like you,' the local party manager confided to her. 'People with experience of conditions abroad will be an asset to the Party.'

Clarissa was flattered. She joined the Party and was unanimously elected secretary of the Paradise Women's Federation. The head of the local branch visited the Forbes often. The rumours circulated. He proposed. Clarissa accepted.

'Your daughter is a terror,' he said to Mr Forbes some time after they had been married. 'A real fanatic about everything local. She does say that she wouldn't even let our children read any of them foreign magazines. Yes man. Clary is a real terror.'

'It take she a long time to learn,' Mr Forbes confessed. 'There was a time . . .'

'I owe it all to my father,' Clarissa interrupted hastily. 'He it is who teach me all I know. He was my first political mentor, right through from my childhood ...' Clarissa elaborated. Her voice drifted sonorously through the sitting room.

Mr Forbes laughed and patted his daughter. He settled back more comfortably into his armchair and as he listened to her conversation, his judgement clouded, but in a manner he was quite content to leave well alone.

Shiva Naipaul

The Beauty
Contest

There were two hardware shops in Doon Town, and the
Oriental Emporium, proprietor R. Prasad, was one of
them. There was nothing remotely oriental about the place,
but the name had been given by Mr Prasad's father (a man
noted for his flights of fancy) and no one cared enough to
change it. The other, just a few doors away, was the more
aptly named General Store, proprietor A. Aleong. Though
selling the same goods, they had succeeded in competing
amicably for many years, and Mr Prasad appeared to
derive a certain pleasure in telling his customers, 'Me and
Mr Aleong is the best of friends. Not a harsh word in ten
years.' But of late relations had cooled. The trouble began
with Stephen Aleong, who had been sent by his father to
study business management in the United States, and had
returned not only with pastel-coloured shirts, but new ideas
as well. The first blow fell when the General Store put up a
neon sign with flickering lights and the picture of a man
dressed cowboy style who said: 'Darn me if this ain't the
finest store in town.' Mrs Prasad agitated for a sign along
similar lines. Her husband was open to new ideas, but
having searched the depths of his imagination he surfaced
with nothing. This tended to happen to Mr Prasad. He
felt that in some inexplicable way, Mr Aleong's sign had
gathered up all the possibilities into itself. The nearest he
had come to success was to have a picture of the Three Wise
Men riding across the desert towards the Oriental Em-

porium, which was to be lit by an ethereal glow. However, he suspected that this, apart from being derivative, was probably also blasphemous, and therefore he adopted an altogether different line of approach.

'The value of my service lies in the quality of the goods I sell,' he told his wife.

'Don't talk stupid man, the both of you does sell the same things.'

'I'm a simple man, Tara, selling to simple people. You think they going to care about neon lights?'

But Mr Prasad had misjudged the simple people. They liked Mr Aleong's neon sign, and there was a perceptible drift of custom away from the Oriental Emporium. Then Mr Aleong did another revolutionary thing. It was the custom in Doon Town for shops to bring their goods on to the pavements, where the bulkier items were displayed. Mr Aleong stopped doing this. 'It lowers the tone of the place,' he explained to Mr Prasad. He renovated the front of the General Store and installed plate-glass windows, behind which the goods were now tastefully arranged by his daughter-in-law. From this alteration a new slogan was born: 'Pavements were made to be walked on.' This caught the public imagination and Mr Prasad's simple people deserted him in ever increasing numbers.

'That man making you look like a fool,' Mrs Prasad told her husband.

'You've got to admit it's original, Tara.' And Mr Prasad, who had recently been more than usually prone to denigrate himself, added, 'I don't know how it is, Tara, but no matter how hard I try I just can't think up original things like that.'

'Pavements made to walk on! You call that original?' Nevertheless, she wondered why it was Mr Aleong and not her husband who had thought of that.

'What are you going to do?' The reproach in her voice was unmistakable. Mr Prasad scratched in vain at the thin top-soil of his imagination.

'Why don't you expand?'

Mr Prasad seemed to be thinking of something else.

'You could buy up Mr Ramnath.' Her expression softened. 'Your trouble is you always under-rating yourself. Think big.'

The idea of expansion appealed to Mr Prasad. He thought big for a few moments, then his face clouded.

'It's a pity how Aleong change really. We used to get on so well together until that sonofabitch son of his begin putting ideas in his head. No fuss, no bother. What do you think get into him?'

'That's business. Aleong is a businessman, he not running a charity on your behalf, and it's high time you realize you was one too. Now what about Mr Ramnath?'

'I don't see how I could do anything there, Tara. Ramnath love he money, hard as nails that man.'

'Think big, man. Stop under-rating yourself.' Mrs Prasad was insistent, suddenly alarmed by the empty spaces she discerned in her own imagination.

'You may be right. Maybe I do under-rate myself.' The cloud lifted. 'I don't know what I would do without you, Tara.'

'Chut, man! You mustn't say things like that.'

They gazed happily at each other.

Mr Ramnath, the owner of the shop next door to the Oriental Emporium, sold chiefly bicycles. He conducted his business with a misanthropic glee which he lavished on colleague and customer alike. Mr Prasad, knowing this, was reluctant to approach him, and his wife had to fan the sinking flames of his ambition for several days beforehand.

Mr Ramnath was standing on the pavement outside his shop when Mr Prasad sidled up to him.

'Good afternoon, Mr Ramnath. I see you taking a little fresh air.'

Mr Ramnath spat amicably on the pavement, and taking out a square of flannel from his pocket, began to polish the handlebars of one of his bicycles.

Mr Prasad coughed sympathetically. 'Look, do you think we can go somewhere where we can talk?'

'What, you in trouble or something?' Mr Ramnath seemed happier suddenly.

'No, no. Nothing like that.' Mr Prasad laughed.

Even Mr Ramnath had his disappointments. He stared gloomily at Mr Prasad. 'Come on inside and tell me about it.'

Mr Ramnath sat on a stool near the cash register on which had been painted in neat black letters: 'We have arranged with the Bank not to give credit. They have agreed not to sell bicycles.'

'It's like this, you see, Mr Ramnath, I want to expand the Emporium . . .'

'Aleong giving you trouble, eh? I was thinking that something like that was bound to happen one of these days.' He brightened, and slapping his thighs let his eye roam fondly over the sign on the register. 'You want my advice?'

Mr Prasad shifted uncomfortably. 'Not your advice so much as . . .'

Mr Ramnath grinned. 'It's the shop you after, not so?'

'You could put it like that.'

'Ten thousand dollars, Mr Prasad, not a penny more, not a penny less.'

'Eh?' Mr Ramnath's alacrity to sell worried him.

'I say ten thousand.'

'You wouldn't consider . . .'

'Ten thousand, Mr Prasad. Not a penny more, not a penny less. This place worth its weight in gold.'

'I'll have to think it over and let you know.'

'That's the way, Mr Prasad; and be quick or I might change my mind.'

'He asking twelve thousand,' Mr Prasad said to his wife. 'It only worth eight.'

'I know. Don't worry, I go beat him down.'

'I can't offer you more than eight, Mr Ramnath.'

'Ten, Mr Prasad. Not a penny more, not a penny less.'

'He's a difficult man to budge, Tara, but I manage to get him down to eleven.'

'That place not worth more than nine.'

'You think I don't know that? Don't worry, I go beat him down.'

'I could offer you nine thousand, Mr Ramnath.'

'You know my answer, Mr Prasad. Not a ...'

'All right, all right.'

'I think I could get him down to ten if I try hard enough, Tara.'

'It's not a bad price when you think about it.'

'I know that. Don't worry, I go beat him down to ten, you wait and see.'

'All right, Mr Ramnath, have it your way. Ten thousand.'

'In cash?'

'Yes, yes, in cash.'

'Consider this place yours, Mr Prasad.'

'Well, he come down to ten.'

'Good man. You see what a little firmness will do? Twelve thousand! Who did he take you for, eh?'

'I told you I could beat him down. All it needed was time.'

But the General Store was not resting on its laurels. The shop assistants appeared in uniform and Mr Aleong retired from the public gaze to the fastnesses of an office at the back of the shop. It was the next move, however, which really shattered the long-standing friendship. Mr Aleong began to cut his prices. Mr Prasad watched helplessly as the General Store, succumbing to a kind of controlled frenzy, announced new give-away offers and bargains each week. His own plans were proceeding feebly. When he had bought out Mr Ramnath his wife's joy had at first known no bounds. The prospect which opened before her promised a shop of palatial grandeur and spiralling profits. She was disappointed. Mr Prasad did not know what to do with the additional space. He demolished the dividing wall and spread his stock more thinly over the enlarged area. The emptiness was embarrassing, and later on he added a few secondhand items. After he had done that his imagination spluttered and died, and his wife's dreams of glory faded. Mr Prasad, sinking deeper into despondency, found fulfilment in prophecies of doom for Mr Aleong, the General Store, and more recently himself.

'Man, I know what you could do,' his wife said one day, visibly excited. 'It's a great idea.'

'What?' The joy of life, never strong in Mr Prasad, seemed to have deserted him entirely.

'You could enter someone for the Miss Doon Town contest. Imagine you get a really nice girl, Miss Oriental Emporium – you know they have to say who sponsoring them in a sash across they chest – and if she win Aleong go come crawling back to you. He'll keep his tail quiet after that.'

'But that need money, Tara, and anyway who go want to be Miss Oriental Emporium?'

'Man, remember what I was telling you. Think big.'

And Mr Prasad did think big, and as he did so a vision of success and revenge rose before him and the fires of hope kindled once again.

If one were to judge by the rancour it aroused, the Carnival Queen contest was without doubt the most important event in Doon Town. The winner was in due course offered up to the National Queen contest, where she had been consigned by tradition to that group of contestants universally acknowledged to have no chance of winning; though their presence there did have one advantage: it gave the other more plausible contestants an occasion to be magnanimous. One year, the national winner, Miss Allied Electrical Traders Ltd, had said afterwards, 'I thought Miss Doon Town looked stunning as Aphrodite,' and Mr Prasad had commented, 'It's she conscience bothering she.' Such lack of grace was understandable. The competition had degenerated into a self-lacerating exercise to which the people of Doon Town felt obliged to submit themselves annually. Mr Prasad, as a member of the town's Chamber of Commerce, took a keen interest in the affair. 'You just wait,' he would say, after Miss Doon Town had made yet another poor showing, 'one day we are going to shock them out of their boots. Let us see who will be laughing then.'

And now, the more he thought about it, the more the conviction took hold of him that it had fallen to him to deliver the people of Doon Town from their bondage. His flights of enthusiasm scaled such heights, that even his wife was worried.

'You forget Aleong. He entering this too, you know,' she reminded him.

'Aleong? Who is Aleong?'

The confidence that comes from a sense of divine protection and mission had descended upon Mr Prasad, and despite herself, his wife was impressed and eventually infected by his fervour.

Mr Prasad discovered in Rita, one of his former shop assistants, the candidate he was looking for. She worked in one of the big department stores in Port-of-Spain. Rita was good looking in the generally accepted way, and her stay in the city had given her 'poise' and 'confidence'. Mr Prasad had no doubts about her suitability while she on her part was eager 'to show Doon a thing or two'.

'But what do you know about this beauty queen business, Mr Prasad?'

He had to confess he knew nothing.

'Well, it got to be done professionally for a start. Professionally.'

'Sure.'

'It's not simply walking across a stage, you know. It takes money and . . . and know-how.'

The transformation in Rita's grammar and vocabulary since she left the Oriental Emporium surprised and unnerved Mr Prasad.

'Don't worry. I ain't going to spare no expense.'

'I know a hairdresser who is experienced in these matters. We better go and see her.'

'Sure, sure. Anything you say.'

Whenever Mr Prasad tried to speak 'properly' he ended up with a mock American accent. He was aware of this and it made him uncomfortable. He left Rita, his sense of mission and divine protection shaken.

The hairdresser was attractive and supercilious. She had been trained in New York.

'So much depends on what you parade as,' she told them. 'From my experience I would say it's either got to be Greek or Roman.' She stared at her long, impeccably polished fingernails. 'Or Egyptian, perhaps. That's quaint.'

Mr Prasad nodded, striving hard to control the threatening American intonations. 'What do you like, Rita? Greek or Roman or Egyptian?'

Rita pondered. 'How about Egyptian? Everybody will be doing something Greek or Roman.'

'You could be Isis for instance,' the hairdresser said.

'What's that? Some kind of god or something?' Mr Prasad asked.

Rita looked embarrassedly out of the window.

'A goddess, Mr Prasad. An ancient Egyptian fertility goddess.'

'You like Isis, Rita?'

'Isis sounds fine to me. It's original.'

'Now there's only one more thing,' the hairdresser held

her fingernails up to the light and squinted at them.
'Do you have any hobbies?'

'I does ... I read a little.'

'We'll use that. What else?'

'To be frank ...'

'Modelling?'

'Well ...'

'We'll use that all the same. Now we must have something quaint or as you would say, original.'

'What's wrong with two hobbies?'

Rita looked out of the window.

'It's *de rigueur* to have three hobbies, Mr Prasad.'

'Try gardening,' the hairdresser suggested.

'But ...'

'No. We'll use gardening. It sounds bohemian. That always helps.'

'What's bohemian?'

'Mr Prasad ...' Rita looked out of the window.

'Well, she going to be Isis,' Mr Prasad informed his wife.

'Who's Isis?'

Mr Prasad was incredulous.

'It's an Egyptian fert ... fertilizer goddess. And she also have three hobbies, reading, modelling and gardening.'

'Gardening?'

'You've got to have something bohemian, you know.'

'Oh.'

Mr Aleong's plans remained wrapped in secrecy. Whereas Mr Prasad splashed the walls of the Oriental Emporium with pictures of Rita and the pyramids and talked incessantly of the competition, the General Store continued to prosper amid a reticence so blatantly discreet that Mr Prasad's conversations gradually assumed a tone at once hysterically boastful and anxious.

'Maybe you shouldn't have advertise it so much,' his

wife said to him, 'That kinda thing does bring bad luck.'

'Bad luck! We go see about that when the time come. But all the same I know that man and he bound to be making mischief somewhere.' He peered at her. 'Do you think he bribing the judges?'

'No man. We would be sure to hear about it if that was the case.'

'All the same.' And the shadows of suspicion chased each other across his face.

However, Mr Aleong appeared to have only the civic virtues on his mind. He issued a pamphlet appealing for 'common-sense and good order' on carnival days, re-iterating what he called his 'unshakable belief in the native tolerance and forbearance' of his fellow citizens. But about his entrant for the contest, not a word. 'He want to be Mayor,' Mr Prasad said.

The contest was held in a cinema. When the Prasads arrived they were conducted to their seats by a girl in mock tropical costume. The Aleongs were late. Mr Aleong smiled pleasantly at Mr Prasad and elbowed his way across to him. 'Well, Mr Prasad, the night we've all been waiting for.'

'Yes. I expect you have a little surprise for us, eh?'

Mr Aleong laughed. 'Oh no, Mr Prasad, nothing like that. For me it's just a bit of fun. I don't suppose you look at it any different yourself?' Mr Aleong patted him on the shoulder. Mrs Prasad frowned.

'The best of luck, old man. Oh, by the way, Mrs Prasad, you look ...' Mr Aleong, waving his arms delightedly, backed away in a cloud of good will.

'The son of a bitch,' Mr Prasad whispered.

There were ten contestants and they were to parade three times: in bathing costume, in evening dress and in a 'costume of the contestant's choice'. The last was crucial. The urbanity of the master of ceremonies, whose presence there was a concession to Doon Town, was paper-thin. His jokes, so successful in Port-of-Spain night clubs, tended to fall flat, and he had even been booed by the audience. The people of Doon Town were not kind.

'And now we come to the first important business of the evening – the parade in bathing costume attire.' The master of ceremonies rocked delicately on his heels as he made the announcement.

The first six girls sauntered across the stage. They looked identical and were evenly applauded.

'Contestant number seven, Miss Ma Fong Restaurant.' Nothing happened.

He glanced hastily at his programme. His professionalism was at stake. 'Miss Ma Fong Restaurant.' Good humour and contempt struggled for dominion over him. He addressed the audience. 'I suppose she take Chinese leave.' They stared at him stony-faced. He grimaced and prodded the back-drop curtain. 'Where is Miss Ma Fong Restaurant?'

At last she appeared, wearing a bikini emblazoned with dragons. The audience gasped, and even the master of ceremonies was unable to control his astonishment. Rita, who came next, seemed pallid by contrast, and Miss General Store, though attractive, was conventional.

The parade in evening dress followed the same pattern, with Miss Ma Fong Restaurant again providing the focus of interest. While the other girls were content to wear eighteenth-century ballgowns, she slithered across the stage in a close-fitting red sheath with a daring slit up the sides. 'The world of Suzie Wong,' the master of ceremonies explained, 'and man, what a world.'

Mr Prasad's impatience melted into irritation. Rita so far had made no impact at all.

'It's that damn Chinaman. They too cunning, I tell you.'

The 'pageantry' (so the programme described it) of the final round unfolded slowly, the goddesses of the Graeco-Roman world following each other in ponderous progression.

Mr. Prasad relaxed.

'These people have no imagination at all. With them it either have to be Greek or Roman. Like they never hear of Egypt at all, but . . .' he turned to his wife, 'they go hear tonight, eh?'

'You getting too excited. Control yourself, man.'

Miss Ma Fong Restaurant was disappointing. Being a Chinese pagoda did not suit her. Anyway, the pagoda was tilting dangerously.

'A Chinese pagoda,' the master of ceremonies intoned. 'From Pisa.'

Again the audience failed to respond. Miss Ma Fong glared at him, and the master of ceremonies, sheltering behind his professionalism, rocked delicately on his heels.

'Miss Oriental Emporium as Isis, the Egyptian fertility goddess.'

There was a rustle of interest. Rita walked circumspectly across the stage, her movements restricted by the shaped tightness of her costume, and the precarious balance of a squat head-dress surmounted by what looked like a pair of bull's horns. In one hand she carried a staff and in the other a scroll of what was presumably 'papyrus'.

'Isis?'

'But I never hear of that one before.' Whispers like these reached Mr Prasad, and he prodded his wife in the ribs and smiled.

'Miss General Store as Fruits and Flowers.'

Mr Prasad stiffened. The audience digested the significance of this before bursting into rapturous applause. Miss General Stores wore what was basically a grass skirt, hidden behind bunches of hibiscus, oleander and carnations. Her bosom and back were encased in banana leaves overspread with wreaths of fern and more flowers, and on her head she balanced a fruit-filled basket from which hung chains of roses reaching to the floor. People rose from their seats and applauded. Someone threw a straw hat on the stage.

'Original!'

'Fruits and flowers, a local thing.'

'Look, she have a real mango and orange.'

The voice of the master of ceremonies rose above the uproar. 'Ladies and gentlemen, you should be here to see this.' He had forgotten he was not on the radio. This time the audience did laugh. Miss General Store tossed a rose into the audience. A man shouted, 'Strip!' She blushed. Everyone knew then that Miss Doon Town would have to be reckoned with in Port-of-Spain that year.

The Prasads left the cinema before the results were announced. They drove home in silence and went to bed. The next morning they read in the paper that Rita had come third. She had hinted in an interview that she would have done better but for her sponsor. She was quoted as saying, 'You must have a professional, not an amateur to look after you in this business.'

When Miss Doon Town came second in the national contest Mr Aleong's fellow citizens expressed their gratitude by electing him their Mayor. His rise in fame was paralleled by a rise in his fortunes. The General Store became one of a chain, Proprietor A. Aleong, and above each of his establishments there blazed forth the slogan, 'The finest store in town'. Mr Prasad, who now owned Doon Town's only secondhand shop, would say, pointing to the General Store, 'Our one claim to fame. You wouldn't believe this, but there was a time when me and Aleong – sorry, I mean the Mayor – used to be good friends. I know it hard to believe what with all them stores and things he own now, but we used to be rivals in the same business. I and that man used to compete. Imagine that!'

He would laugh for a long time after he said this, but there was no unhappiness or regret in that laugh. Mr Prasad was content. After all, the Oriental Emporium *was* the only secondhand shop in Doon Town.

Isaac Babel

Inspiration

I wanted to sleep, and I was in a bad mood. Just then
Mishka came to read his story. 'Shut the door,' he said
and pulled a bottle of wine out of his pocket.

'This is my day. I've finished my story. I think it's the
real thing. Let's have a drink on it, friend.'

Mishka's face was pale and sweaty.

'People who say there's no such thing as happiness are
fools,' he said. 'Happiness is inspiration. I wrote all last
night and didn't notice the dawn come. Then I walked
around the town. The town is extraordinary, early in the
morning: dew, silence, and very few people. Everything is
crystal-clear and you can see the day coming: cold and
blue, ghostly and gentle. Let's drink, friend. I'm as sure
as sure can be: this story's a turning point in my life.'
Mishka poured himself some wine and drank. His fingers
quivered. He had a hand of remarkable beauty – slender,
white, and smooth, with tapering fingers.

'You know, I must place this story,' he went on. 'They'll
take it anywhere. They print such rubbish nowadays. The
main thing is to have some pull. I've had a promise. Sukhotin will fix everything ...'

'Mishka,' I said, 'You should go through it again –
nothing's crossed out ...'

'To hell with it – plenty of time for that. ... At home,
you know, they just make fun of me. *Rira bien qui rira le
dernier*. I don't say a thing, you know. In a year's time we

shall see what we shall see. They'll come crawling . . .'
The bottle was nearly empty.

'Stop drinking, Mishka . . .'

'I have to pep myself up,' he replied. 'Last night I smoked forty cigarettes.' He took out an exercise book. It was very thick, very thick indeed. I played with the idea of asking him to leave it with me. But then I looked at his pale forehead, on which a vein had swollen up, at his wretched, twisted necktie, and I said: 'Very well, Leo Tolstoy . . . when you write your autobiography, remember me . . .'

Mishka smiled. 'Bastard,' he replied. 'You don't value my friendship at all.'

I settled myself comfortably. Mishka bent over his exercise book. The room was quiet and half in darkness.

'In this story,' Mishka said, 'I have tried to do something new, something shrouded in a haze of wonder, full of tenderness, half shades, and allusiveness . . . I am utterly sick of the crassness of our life . . .'

'Cut out the preliminaries,' I said. 'Start reading . . .'

He began. I listened attentively. It was not easy: the story was bad and boring. A salesclerk had fallen in love with a ballerina and spent all his time hanging about under her window. She went away and the salesclerk was upset because his dream of love had been disappointed.

Soon I stopped listening. The words in the story were boring, hackneyed, and smooth, like polished wooden counters. Nothing came through: what sort of a fellow the salesclerk was, what she was like.

I looked at Mishka. His eyes were on fire. He ground his cigarettes, as they went out, between his fingers. His dull face which had been grievously narrowed and needlessly foreshortened in the making, his large, protruding, yellow nose, his swollen, pale-pink lips – they all grew brighter and slowly, with steadily mounting force, filled with the joyfully self-confident flush of creativity.

He read with agonizing slowness and when he had finished, he clumsily pocketed the exercise book and looked at me. . . .

'You see, Mishka,' I said slowly, 'you see, this needs some thought. . . . The idea is very original, and the tenderness comes through . . . but you see, the way you've written it . . . . It'll have to be polished a little, you know . . .'

'I've been working on this thing for three years,' Mishka replied. 'There are some rough bits, of course, but taken as a whole . . .'

Something had gotten home to him. His lip trembled. He hunched his shoulders and took an awful long time to light a cigarette.

'Mishka,' I said, 'it's a wonderful thing you've written. You're still a little short on technique, but *ça viendra*. My God, what a lot you've got in that head of yours . . .'

Mishka turned around and looked at me. His eyes were like a child's: loving, bright and happy.

'Let's go out,' he said. 'It's stuffy in here.'

The streets were dark and silent.

Mishka pressed my hand hard and said: 'I'm as sure as sure can be: I have talent. My father wants me to find a job. I'm not saying a thing. In autumn it's Petrograd for me. Sukhotin will fix everything.'

He paused, lit a new cigarette from the previous one, and went on more quietly: 'Sometimes I feel such inspiration it hurts. Then I know that what I'm doing is right. I sleep badly – nightmares all the time and feeling really miserable. I turn over and over for three hours in bed before I get to sleep. In the morning my head aches with a terrible, dull kind of pain. I can only write at night, when there's nobody around and it's quiet, and I'm all on fire. Dostoevsky always wrote at night and drank tea by the samovar while he was at it, but I have my cigarettes. . . . You should just see the smoke in my room . . .'

We reached Mishka's home. His face was caught in the light of a street lamp. An eager, thin, sallow, and happy face it was.

'We'll show 'em, God damn it!' he said and squeezed my hand even more tightly. 'In Petrograd everybody makes it.'

'All the same, Mishka,' I said, 'one has to work . . .'

'Sashka, my friend,' he replied with a broad and condescending smile, 'I'm no fool – I know what's what. Don't worry, I'm not resting on my laurels. Come by tomorrow, we'll take another look.'

'All right,' I said, 'I'll come.'

We said good night. I went back home. It was all very depressing.

Biographical Notes

Sean O'Faolain

born in Cork, Ireland, in 1900 and educated at the National University of Ireland, served in the Irish Republican Army for six years, taught, then studied for three years at Harvard University, and later in Italy. 'At Harvard', he says, 'I learned most uncomfortably that facts are facts. In Italy I learned that facts are the way you look at them.' He has written some twenty books including travel, literary criticism, novels and biographies, but is most famous for his stories. He is married, with two children, and lives in County Dublin. His wife has written several books of Irish folk tales and his daughter Julia published her first book of stories in 1968.

Nadine Gordimer

born in Springs, a gold mining town on the East Rand in South Africa, went to Witwatersrand University, started writing when still a child and published stories in the children's supplement of the biggest newspaper in Johannesburg. Since her first impressive collection of stories, *The Soft Voice of the Serpent*, in 1949 she has written eight books, and in 1961 her story collection *Friday's Footprint* received the W. H. Smith Literary Award and was listed by the *New York Times* among the 200 best works of fiction in the world. Her latest novel, *Late Bourgeois World*, is banned in South Africa where she still lives and writes, believing with Sartre that 'by going into exile, no matter how good the reasons are for doing so, one loses one's place in the world and can never quite recover it again'.

Shiva Naipaul

born in Port-of-Spain, Trinidad, in 1945, is the younger brother of the distinguished novelist V. S. Naipaul. In 1964 he went up to Oxford to read philosophy and psychology but took his degree in Chinese instead. He began writing just before finals. This is his first appearance in print. 'The Beauty Contest' was the first story he wrote; 'Man of Mystery' the second. His novel *Fireflies* will be published later this year.

Isaac Babel

born 1894 in Odessa into a lower middle-class Russian Jewish family, went to St Petersburg when he was 21 where he lived in great poverty, but was helped by Gorky, who published two of his stories. During the revolution and civil war he held a series of minor posts, joined the Red Army and fought with the cavalry. His first stories were immediately successful and encouraged him to publish *Odessa Tales* in 1924 and *Red Cavalry* in 1926. Other stories, scenarios and plays followed, but by 1934 Babel had come to describe himself ironically as 'the master of the genre of silence'. In 1939 he was arrested. It is believed that he died in 1941.

More about Penguins

Penguinews, which appears every month, contains details of all the new books issued by Penguins as they are published. From time to time it is supplemented by *Penguins in Print*, which is a complete list of all books published by Penguins which are in print. (There are well over three thousand of these.)

A specimen copy of *Penguinews* will be sent to you free on request, and you can become a subscriber for the price of the postage. For a year's issues (including the complete lists) please send 4s. if you live in the United Kingdom, or 8s. if you live elsewhere. Just write to Dept EP, Penguin Books Ltd, Harmondsworth, Middlesex, enclosing a cheque or postal order, and your name will be added to the mailing list.

Some other books published by Penguins are described on the following pages.
Note: *Penguinews* and *Penguins in Print* are not available in the U.S.A. or Canada

The Irish

Sean O'Faolain

Revised and Enlarged Edition

'A creative history of the growth of a racial mind' – this is Sean O'Faolain's own description of a book in which he has no truck with political events, wars, or rebellions and rejects the popular Irish notion of 'seven hundred years of slavery'.

Many racial, religious, social, and intellectual strands have, over the centuries, been woven into the cloth of Irish genius, and it is Sean O'Faolain's achievement to have disentangled these in a study which first appeared as a Pelican over twenty years ago and has now been largely re-written. The wild, imaginative, disunited Ireland of the Celts, which for years became the fountainhead of Christianity; the intrusion of Danes and Normans, who defied the Irish horror of towns and began to urbanize the island; the years of English ascendancy, when new populations and a new language were planted; the upsurge of Irish nationalism and Irish letters after 1800 – all these Sean O'Faolain records, critically and engagingly.

Finally he distinguishes six representative types which have branched from the Tree of Liberty – the new peasantry, the Anglo-Irish, the rebels, the priests, the writers, and the politicians.

Not for sale in the U.S.A.

A World of Strangers

Nadine Gordimer

Nadine Gordimer is a leading South African novelist and short story writer.

In *A World of Strangers* a young Englishman is sent out to Johannesburg to represent a publishing firm. His friendships with Afrikaners and Africans make him aware of the completely separate worlds of the many races there and their grim struggle for existence.

'A subtle and cunning study of her country's racial problem. First-class' – *Star*

'An astonishingly brilliant book' – *Daily Telegraph*
'Stunningly good' – *Tatler*

'An admirable, highly intelligent and adult novel' – *Sunday Times*

Not for sale in Canada and the U.S.A.

South African Writing Today

Edited by Nadine Gordimer and Lionel Abrahams

This collection of the best recent South African poetry, prose, and drama has been made without regard for differences of colour or race and shows the strength of South African writing today.

Fireflies

Shiva Naipaul

Raised by her fearsome great-aunt, the guardian of the Khoja family's considerable fortunes and even greater self-importance, Mrs Lutchman is cast adrift at the age of eighteen into marriage with a capricious and unsuccessful man. This is the story of her life, which is given a touching dignity by her innate sense of duty and her generosity of heart. It is also the story of the Khoja's decline, and it is they who provide the rich comic detail which prevents this novel from being a sad one. The clan's belief in its own grandeur breeds splendid eccentricities, shrewdly and lovingly observed, and its ramifications extend so far into the life of Trinidad that finally a whole society frames the portrait of the family, just as the whole family frames the portrait of Mrs Lutchman. Few novelists attempt so much in a first book, and it is hard to think of any who have brought it off so triumphantly as Shiva Naipaul.

Not for sale in the U.S.A.

Also in Penguin Modern Stories

There are today so few serious publications devoted to
the short story that there is no need, in introducing
Penguin Modern Stories, to say more than that we believe in
the short story, know that a great many of the best
contemporary writers are working in this form, and look
forward to publishing many well-known authors as well
as introducing many new ones in this quarterly series.
All these stories are published here for the first time in
this country.

Volume 1 contains stories by William Sansom, Jean Rhys,
David Plante and Bernard Malamud.*

Volume 2 contains stories by John Updike, Sylvia Plath
and Emanuel Litvinoff.*

Volume 3 contains stories by Philip Roth, Margaret
Drabble, Jay Neugeboren, and Giles Gordon.

Not for sale in Canada or the U.S.A.
**Not for sale in the U.S.A.*